Karl felt his rag 'olack had begun to br ınger, too. Even Ami, unted and cleared his t

Creeping Jesus nen's anger. He snap] our of being fighting soldiers, I am sending the lot of you back to the kitchens, where undoubtedly *Oberfeldwebel* Bulle will ensure, at least, that you work – and work hard – until the Colonel decides you have earned the privilege of returning to the ranks of the grenadiers. Now get out of my sight! I can't stand your stupid, cowardly faces any longer . . .'

Also by Leo Kessler

The *SS Assault Regiment Wotan* Series

SS PANZER BATTALION
DEATH'S HEAD
CLAWS OF STEEL
GUNS AT CASSINO
THE DEVIL'S SHIELD
HAMMER OF THE GODS
FORCED MARCH
BLOOD AND ICE
THE SAND PANTHERS
COUNTER-ATTACK
PANZER HUNT
SLAUGHTER GROUND
HELLFIRE
FLASHPOINT
CAULDRON OF BLOOD
SCHIRMER'S HEADHUNTERS
WHORES OF WAR
SCHIRMER'S DEATH LEGION
SLAUGHTER AT SALERNO
MARCH OR DIE

The *Submarine* Series

THE WOLF PACK
OPERATION DEATH WATCH
CONVOY TO CATASTROPHE

The *Stormtroop* Series

STORMTROOP
BLOOD MOUNTAIN
VALLEY OF THE ASSASSINS
RED ASSAULT
HIMMLER'S GOLD
FIRE OVER KABUL
WAVE OF TERROR
EAGLES IN THE SNOW
FIRE OVER AFRICA

The *Otto Stahl* Series

OTTO'S PHONEY WAR
OTTO'S BLITZKRIEG!
OTTO AND THE REDS
OTTO AND THE YANKS
OTTO AND THE SS
OTTO AND THE HIMMLER LOVE LETTERS

LEO KESSLER

Cannon Fodder

Rebel 1

Futura

A Futura Book

First published in Great Britain in 1986
by Century Hutchinson Ltd, London

This edition published in 1987
by Futura Publications, a Division of
Macdonald & Co (Publishers) Ltd
London & Sydney

*All characters in this publication are fictitious
and any resemblance to real persons, living or dead,
is purely coincidental.*

ISBN 0 7088 3450 7

Printed and bound in Great Britain by
Collins, Glasgow

Futura Publications
A Division of
Macdonald & Co (Publishers) Ltd
Greater London House
Hampstead Road
London NW1 7QX

A BPCC plc Company

'He who eats with the Devil needs a long spoon.'

Old German saying

PRELUDE

The Making of a Rebel

'Love drove me to rebel. Love drives me back to grope with them through Hell.'

Siegfried Sassoon

CARSTENS, Karl. B.1920, Hamburg-Billstedt. Education: Billstedt-Volksschule. Occupation: Slater and Tiler. Mustered for the Wehrmacht, 1939. Assigned to the Fourth Grenadier Regiment – 'the Crown Prince's Own'.

They had come for the old man just after he had arrived home on his bike from work. Four of them in ankle-length green leather coats which creaked when they moved and felt hats pulled down low over their faces like detectives in the movies. All of them had been chewing on dark stumps of cigars. Afterwards, when Karl came to see more of them, he had fancied those coats and cigars were their trade-marks. All of them seemed to wear and smoke the damned things.

Wordlessly they had pushed by his mother, frying her potatoes for the *Bauernfruhstück** on the coal stove. They eyed the old Bebel saying on the kitchen wall – '*Man of work, all the wheels stand still, if your strong arm wills it*' – grunted contemptuously, then crooked a finger at the old man sitting on the sofa, face suddenly very pale. '*Mitkommen*!' the Gestapo inspector had grunted. That was all.

As soon as they had him outside, they had begun to beat him up in a stolid, routine sort of way. Without any malice. It was just another arrest. The way they always treated political prisoners.

For that was what the old man was now. A political prisoner! The old fool had remained loyal to the SPD**, even though the leadership had long since fled abroad, to England and Sweden, and the party's members had gone over to the triumphant Nazis by their thousands and tens of thousands

*'Farmer's breakfast', a dish consisting of fried potatoes, bacon and eggs.

**German socialist party.

back in 1933. The silly old fart had been distributing crappy leaflets down by Dammtor station, illegal, of course, all about the price of butter under the Nazis and that kind of bull. As if anybody cared? Besides, when had the average Hamburg working-class family ever eaten damned butter?

They had allowed him and his Mama to see the old man one last time before they set off to Neuengamme Concentration Camp, where they had police dogs trained to bite the balls off unruly prisoners and where the guards toted whips made of bull's pizzles.

Mama had cried all the time, throwing her apron up into her face as if she wanted to blot out everything. But the old man hadn't attempted to console her. His whole attention had been directed on Karl, as if he were seeing his son for the very first time. By now most of the old man's teeth had gone, and his right ear was swollen to twice its normal size. His right eye was almost closed too. But the fear had vanished from his tough old unshaven face and there was determination in his voice as he whispered to Karl, 'Never serve them, Karl, *never*, promise me, my son!' He had seized Karl's hand and had pressed it fervently with his big heavy slater's paw.

Karl didn't need to be told who 'they' were. They were the Nazis. The loud-mouthed, fat-bellied, middle-class grocers and clerks strutting around in their brown boots and uniforms, showing off the medals they had won in the Old War, shoving other people off the pavements, getting drunk and wrecking Jewish shops. Yes, he knew *them* all right!

Abruptly he had been seized by a fierce love for the battered old man squatting opposite him on the three-legged stool under the naked light bulb, with the fat warder watching suspiciously from the barred door. He had returned that grip and had whispered with equal fervour, his handsome young face set and grim, 'Don't worry, Papa, *I'll never serve them. . .*'

ZIMANSKI, Ludwik, nicknamed 'Polack' Born 1919, Altstadt, West Prussia. Education, Altstadt Volksschule and the Holy Virgin of

Cracow Convent School. Occupation: farm labourer. Volunteered for the Fourth Grenadier Regiment. 1939.

One day after the *Wehrmacht* had smashed its way across the Polish border, they had arrived in the village, cheered by those who could still cheer. For they had been cheering and waving the new flags for over twenty-four hours now *by order*, ever since they had been 'liberated' at four the previous morning.

There had been two of them in black uniform. One was immensely fat and completely bald, his face glazed with sweat. The other was emaciated and wan, wearing a thick uniform greatcoat complete with swastika armband and gloves, despite the heat of the day. '*Boshe moi*,' his friend Anton had whispered, as the young men of the village were herded into to the little old schoolhouse, 'They just look like *dick und doof*.'*

With a self-important air the two strode inside, the bare boards creaking under the fat one's tread, past the yellowing photographs of school groups of long ago: shaven-headed boys and long-haired girls in white aprons, grouped around pot-bellied teachers with Kaiser Wilhelm moustaches.

The fat one had done most of the talking and his contempt for the young male villagers who had been hurriedly rounded up by an anxious burgomaster an hour before, was all too obvious. 'Comrades,' he had barked, hands on fat hips, booted feet astride, as if he were Hitler addressing a Party rally, 'you now have the honour of being German again. Thanks to our glorious and ever victorious *Wehrmacht*, West Prussia is once more part of the Reich!'

He had paused, as if he half expected applause, perhaps even an outburst of 'Heil Hitlers', but he had been disappointed. '*Heil*,' Weber, who was a real German, had muttered uncertainly, but that was all. The remaining village youths had remained stubbornly silent at the great news.

'Half breeds . . . Water-Poles!' the thin one had sneered angrily, a dewdrop trembling at the end of his pointed nose. 'Border pack!'

*Fat and Stupid, the German names for Laurel and Hardy.

'But, comrades, the privilege of being German,' the fat one continued, face stern and masterful now, 'is attended by responsibilities. Our Führer, Adolf Hitler, cannot shoulder the burden alone, great man that he is!'

Later Polack could have sworn the fat one's eyes had flooded with tears at that particular moment.

'Now already, comrades, the Führer's brave SS have suffered serious losses in their battle against the Polish sub-humans. How many of our brave boys have been shot in the back by those treacherous Slavs? Some of their prisoners, we have heard, were tortured to death, with their manhood cut off, or fed through a saw, a *circular* saw! That is the kind of person your Polack is, *treacherous, perverted, decadent*!'

He spat out each word furiously, while his companion nodded his head in righteous agreement, the dewdrop trembling at the tip of his nose, both of them apparently unaware of the mood of smouldering anger among these men, German by law, but Polish by descent. Indeed, everyone there - save Weber - had a relative currently fighting the German invaders in the Polish Army.

'So, comrades, we have come here to make you this great offer,' the fat one concluded, eyes beaming at them like a successful door-to-door salesman. 'This day, providing you pass the mustering board, for the Führer's elite must be in peak condition,' he raised his fat finger in warning, 'you are being granted the honour of serving in the Führer's own regiment - *the Adolf Hitler Bodyguard . . . ! The SS itself*!'

'*The SS*,' the dreaded initials had been whispered from man to man. Standing next to Polack Anton had crossed himself hastily and hissed. '*Never!* The priest would never confess me again if I joined those godless heathens!'

Polack, big, slow and darkly handsome in a Slavic way, nodded his agreement. Even in Altstadt they had heard about the SS.

'Now then,' the thin man snapped, stepped forward to the front of the rostrum, while the fat one refreshed himself from a silver hip flask, 'step forward, one at a time and give me your name, address, and age.'

No one moved!

The thin one stared at the young village men aghast. 'Did you not hear? Hey, you, the big one,' he pointed at Polack, 'step up here and give me your particulars at once!'

Polack felt himself flushing a deep embarrassed red, but still he did not move. A heavy silence fell on the group. Outside there was the sound of more troops moving to the front, the clatter of tanks and infantry slogging through the white dust of the village street.

The thin one nodded to the other one. Almost casually he sauntered forward, his fat back trembling, and locking the schoolhouse door pocketed the key with an air of finality.

'All right, you border pack,' the thin one snapped. 'No one is leaving this room before he has signed up for the SS. You Polack pigs, here we are handing you the opportunity on a silver platter to become real Germans, and not Slavic shit-shovellers, and you turn it down. Heaven, arse and cloudburst!' he burst out, no longer able to contain his rage at these stubborn peasants. 'Either join here and now, or damnwell go to the camps –'

Polack's sickle caught him directly in the centre of his forehead. He went reeling back, the curved farm instrument sticking grotesquely from his head, to slam against the wall. For a moment he simply hung there stupidly, dying on his feet, then he started to trail down the wall, leaving a bright scarlet smear behind him to slump on the floor, dead.

'*Run, Ludwik. For God's sake, run for it*!' Anton yelled, as the fat one fumbled for his pistol.

Polack needed no urging. He went through the window in a spectacular dive, sending flying glass everywhere. Next moment he was running all out, down the village street, scattering startled German infantry to left and right. Twenty-four hours later he took a dive; it seemed the only way to escape from the vengeance of the SS. He enlisted in the Fourth Grenadier Regiment . . .

DOEPGEN, Adolf Steven, known as 'Ami'. B. 1920, Koblenz-

Guels. Education: Guels Volksschule and Koblenz Central Catholic Orphanage School. Occupation: Journeyman-Baker. Mustered for the Wehrmacht 1939. Assigned to the Fourth Grenadier Regiment.

'*Steven*?' they would query the first time they met him. 'That ain't a real German name is it?'

He would tell them, shame-faced, that it was his father's name and as always, there came the old reaction, a mixture of surprise and contempt. 'Then you must be one of those Occupation Army bastards – *an Ami*!'

They had said it in the village school. Later in the orphanage where they had sent him after his mother had died, it had been the same. They had said it too at Fleischmann's Bakery, when he had commenced his apprenticeship; and naturally the brown bastards, the Nazis, had taken a special delight in taunting him – 'A miss for a mother and an Ami for a father. Not the kind of person we need in our New Germany!'

'*Ami . . . Ami . . . Ami . . .*' That name had accompanied him throughout his short life. Teachers, schoolmates, nuns, bosses, Nazis – the whole rotten lot of them had taunted him with it for as long as he could remember. How often had he cried himself to sleep because of it. But he had become hard too. If the New Order, this vaunted 1,000 Year Reich, didn't want him, then he didn't want it either.

Smart, quick, blessed with a lot of that Rhenish cunning and perhaps some of his unknown American father's doggedness and independence as well, Adolf Steven Doepgen, known as 'Ami', knew now, as the State demanded his body as cannonfodder for Adolf Hitler, that there was only one thing for him to do – *survive* . . .

Thus, as yet unknown to one another, these three young men journeyed from the furthest corners of the Reich to join their new regiment. They hated the brown-uniformed vulgar pomp and savagery of a Germany which was soon to create the greatest empire the world had seen since the days of the Romans. Yet they would be forced to serve it, however unwillingly; even to become the goulash cannon heroes, until in the end time ran out for National Socialist Germany – and for them. . .

BOOK ONE

The Initiation

'Gentlemen-rankers out on a spree
Damned from here to Eternity
God ha' mercy on such as we,
Ba! Yah! Bah!'

Rudyard Kipling

CHAPTER 1

SMARTLY THE helmeted sentry threw up the red-and-white striped pole. The truck driver rammed home first gear. The recruits crowded in the back on the freezing vehicle stumbled and clutched for support. Slowly the truck started to crawl into the parade ground of the *Adolf Hitler Kaserne*, its cobbles a glittering white in the morning hoar-frost.

Soldiers in shapeless white fatigues were everywhere: crawling on their bellies under the scornful gaze of barrel-chested NCOs; doubling back and forth, red-faced and sweating, their breath fogging a dark-grey in the icy air; kneeling and taking pot-shots with unloaded rifles; standing rigidly to attention, eyes fixed woodenly on the hard-blue winter horizon, saluting some imaginary general. All was hectic, harsh movement, punctuated by the stamp of steel-shod boots and the staccato bark of the non-commissioned officers, who stood there in the glittering square beneath the blood-red flag of the New Germany as if they had been planted.

'Frigging toy soldiers,' Polack growled scornfully in that oddly accented German of his. 'Shit sez the King and a thousand assholes bent and took the strain for in them days, the word of the King was law!' His dark, pear-shaped Slavic face contorted and he spat contemptuously over the tail-gate.

Karl jabbed his elbow into the big Pole's side and hissed, 'Trap, Polack! Shut yer trap!' He pointed to the black silhouette of a sinister-looking man painted on the wall opposite with below it the legend, '*SSSH! THE ENEMY MIGHT BE LISTENING*!'

Next to him the third of the 'Rebels', as they liked to call themselves, Ami, nodded his head wisely and agreed: 'Trust nobody these days, that's my motto. Trust nobody.'

Polack spat again contemptuously, as a heavy hand slapped against the canvas and the fat corporal who had collected them at the station growled, 'All right, you bunch o' piss-pansies, let's be havin' yer. At the double now! Jesus Christ hissen is heading straight this way. Come on, now . . . Move them frigging sow-asses of yourn!'

Stiffly the recruits began to drop over the side, hauling their packs and rifles with them, tugging at their uniforms, pulling their glittering new helmets straight, as fifty metres away an elegant officer, who was actually carrying a sword, began to bear down on them, his gaze under the polished cap peak fixed on some distant horizon known only to himself.

Ami looked at Karl, who had 'big city' written all over his handsome, keen young face, and hissed out of the side of his mouth, 'Yer can see why they call him Jesus Christ, Karl, can't yer?'

Karl nodded and tugged hard at his tunic. 'That you can, Ami. He must think he's walking over the frigging water!'

Polack, who towered above the rest of them, his helmet squatting on the top of his shaven skull like a child's toy, frowned darkly and said, 'You shouldn't talk like that about Our Lord. It ain't right to take His Name in vain, Karl.' In spite of his rugged personality, the big Pole went to church regularly every Sunday, shrugging off all the snide remarks made by his comrades in recruit training.

Karl grinned and Ami, who came from the Catholic Rhineland himself, sneered, 'You know what those lads who wear frocks on Sunday do, don't yer, Polack?' He made an obscene rubbing gesture with his right hand and moaned as if in sexual ecstasy.

Polack clenched a fist like a small steam hammer. 'any more of that, you little ape-turd,' he growled, 'and you'll be lacking a set of teeth –'

'Stop that talking in the ranks, will you?' the fat corporal barked, his breath fogging the cold air, his nickel-rimmed glasses beginning to steam up. 'Officer on parade. Draft . . . draft, *attention*!'

As one the new recruits stamped to attention, their steel-shod boots slamming down on the glistening cobbles, as the fat corporal swung up his hand in a tremendous salute to bellow: 'One corporal, fifty grenadiers all present and correct, *sir*!'

Slowly, terribly slowly, Captain von Schorr, Adjutant to the Fourth Grenadier Regiment, known behind his elegant back as 'Jesus Christ' or even more commonly as 'Creeping Jesus', raised his gloved hand to his cap. 'Thank you, Corporal,' he said languidly in an affected military drawl, 'you have my permission to stand the men at ease.' He yawned and raised his left hand to his lips, as if this was all very much of a bore.

The fat corporal rapped out an order. The men of the draft, laden like pack animals with their equipment, thrust out their right feet in the position of ease, and waited. Captain von Schorr let them wait. He always believed, as he often told his cronies in the officers' mess, in putting the men firmly in their place from the very start. 'Like well-trained gundogs, you know, chaps. Know who their master is and come to heel the instant they are called by him, what!'

Now, slowly, the Adjutant, with his weak. chinless face and tightly corsetted waist, appeared to become aware of them. He had a look of distaste as if he didn't particularly like what he saw in front of him this icy December morning. He screwed the monocle he affected more firmly in his eye, and said: 'You have been greatly honoured by being posted to the Fourth Grenadier Regiment, formerly known in the Old Army as the 'Crown Prince's Own', a regiment whose glorious traditions go back to the eighteenth century when. . .'

Karl frowned as 'Creeping Jesus' droned on in his silly affected manner. Even Hitler and the Nazis had not been able to eradicate the old Imperialist traditions, which his father had hated so much, it seemed. But then, as his old man had always maintained, before the Gestapo had finally dragged him off to Neuengamme* for good, the Army was a 'law unto itself and never you forget it, young Karl. You've got to get up early in the morning, if you want to outsmart the

*An early concentration camp near Hamburg.

soldiers. Mark my words, my boy, they'll have yer turnip shot right off yer shoulders, if you don't watch them buggers!' The handsome young soldier's frown deepened even more and his bright blue honest eyes flashed fire, as he promised his missing father they weren't going to shoot off his 'turnip', come what may, *no sir*!

'So,' Creeping Jesus was saying, while the men of the new draft slowly began to turn blue with the freezing cold, 'it is indeed an honour to be posted to such an illustrious regiment as the Fourth Grenadiers. But remember,' he raised one elegantly gloved hand in warning, 'it is an honour which has to be earned. In due course, our Führer will attack and destroy the decadent French over there,' vaguely he indicated the snow-covered Vosges mountains on the horizon which were in France, 'and you will undoubtedly be allowed to sacrifice your lives for Folk, Fatherland, and Führer – *and the Fourth Grenadiers*! But before that glorious day, you must be trained in the traditions of the Fourth, worthy of that death on the field of battle which, God willing, will be your lot!'

Next to Karl, his face set and angry now at the realization that Creeping Jesus regarded them simply as more cannon-fodder, Polack gave a low contemptuous fart. But if Creeping Jesus heard, his face showed no sign of it. Instead he rasped, 'All right, Corporal, wheel them away. Fatigues for the first week before we start training them to be grenadiers!'

The fat corporal sprang to attention, throwing the adjutant a tremendous salute so that his jowls quivered with the effort, bellowing out orders at the same time. But Creeping Jesus had already turned and seemed to be floating across the parade ground with everyone automatically getting out of his way. Not that he noticed. Obviously he took it as part of his aristocratic birthright that these inferior mortals should not hinder his godlike progress.

The fat corporal relaxed a little, as the Adjutant disappeared from sight. 'Let me give you a bit o' advice, you bunch o' cardboard soldiers,' he said softly, eyes behind the army-issue glasses gentle now. 'There are three real assholes in this regiment. The first is the colonel, who is dotty, absolutely *meschugge*! Got birds in *his* belfry which go tweet-tweet all the time.' He sighed, as if sorely tried. 'If anyone's gonna make heroes of you lot by getting yer frigging well killed, it'll be Colonel frigging von Heinersdorff. Watch him!'

'The next asshole is the one you've just met – *Creeping Jesus*! Now he don't want to become a hero, at least not when the shit's flying in *his* direction. We old hares all saw that back in Poland. That particular asshole'd sacrifice his own mother – if he had one – to save his upperclass hide.'

The fat corporal paused. Behind him on the square a group of recruits were hopping across the cobbles, rifles extended, chivvied all the while by the instructors, faces purple with the effort, like grotesque dirty-white penguins. '*Come on*,' the sergeant in charge cried raucously, '*don't drag them asses! Open yer frigging legs . . . nothing'll fall out . . . And if it does, I'll pick 'em up personally. Come on now . . . move!*'

'The third asshole is the biggest one o' the frigging lot!' the fat corporal continued. 'Like the colonel, I think, he's not got all his cups in the cupboard half the frigging time. He's out to save his precious hide, too, just like Creeping Jesus – if anybody's gonna survive this war, it's gonna be him.' The fat corporal lowered his voice significantly. 'Worst of all though, this particular asshole steals the troops' rations. They say he's made –'

'*What's all that frigging chat going on over there?*' A tremendous voice cut into the corporal's revelations, making the recruits jump, its echo booming back and forth across the big parade ground.

Automatically Karl swung round in time to catch a glimpse of little piglike suspicious eyes set in a broad, brick-red face, as the fat corporal choked, 'Oh, my aching backside, it's him. The third asshole . . . *It's King Bull* . . .'

CHAPTER 2

'Crud! Creeping crap-assed cripples! Clapped-out crocks of careless crap! Crab-infested, crook-donged, crawling, creepy cunts . . .'

That tremendous voice swept through the great steaming kitchen, making the gleaming pots tremble on the hods and the tin plates rattle in the shelves, as that litany of utter contempt poured from the huge sergeant's lips. The recruits in their white fatigues quivered and quailed under that massive, unexpected onslaught. Next to Karl, Ami looked as if he might faint at any moment. Even Polack, the imperturbable member of the Rebels, was awed by that ear-splitting volume of sound that poured from the NCO, who in his gleaming white tunic adorned by the Iron Cross and the Poland Victory Medal, was at least half a head taller than himself.

The huge head cook sucked in a huge gulp of air, massive chest threatening to burst the gleaming buttons of his tunic at any moment.

Ami swayed drunkenly and Karl caught him just in time, thanking a God he no longer believed it that the noise had ceased for a moment. Polack cursed in Polish.

The head cook smiled triumphantly, as he towered above the dazed fatigue-men, hands like small steam shovels on his broad hips, pig-like eyes peering down at them, as if he knew their innermost secrets. Next to him, the lantern-jawed corporal whose skin shone over his cheekbones like wax, stood poised with his notebook at the ready. He had heard it all before. In a minute work would start and he would be needed.

'*Who am I?*' the head cook bellowed suddenly.

They replied as one, for the lantern-jawed corporal named Tietze had briefed them before. 'You are the Bull, Sergeant . . . *King Bull*!'

'You've got it!' the head cook bellowed proudly, swelling

out his chest. 'I am King Bull, in charge of the kitchens of the Fourth Grenadier Regiment.' He poked a finger like a hairy sausage at his chest. 'Here *my* word is law. Here *I* have the say and nobody else. If I say, stick yer dong up yer ass and give yersen a cheap thrill,' he grinned evilly, 'yer do it and complain to the chaplain afterwards. If I sez stick yer pinkies in a pan of boiling water to test if it's hot, yer put yer frigging pinkies in the water. The bone-menders can allus patch yer up later.'

He paused for breath, chest heaving, his red-rimmed eyes glittering dangerously. A worried Karl told himself that the fat corporal had been right. King Bull, like the dotty regimental colonel, didn't have all his cups in his cupboard. He was a man to be watched and treated with kid gloves.

'Remember this, then, you bunch of wet-tails,' King Bull continued, fixing them with those evil eyes of his, 'this is King Bull's kingdom and my rule is absolute.' Slowly, significantly, he took a whistle attached to a gleaming brass chain from the right pocket of his white tunic. 'My whistle, King Bull's whistle,' he announced, emphasising the words as if they were very important. 'One blast on this whistle and you are in trouble. *What are you?*' he demanded.

'*We're in trouble!*' they chanted hastily, like a bunch of frightened schoolchildren repeating their lesson for some feared teacher, already swishing his cane up and down menacingly.

King Bull beamed happily, but his little eyes didn't light up; they remained as suspicious as ever. 'Two blasts on this whistle and you're in serious trouble. *What are you?*'

'*We're in serious trouble!*' their young voices cried dutifully.

King Bull paused dramatically, while Karl experienced a sinking feeling. Recruit training had been hell and he had consoled himself that a posting to a unit stationed in what was really the front, though not a single shot had yet been fired in anger here, would be different: the threats, the ugly harassment and constant bullying would end. But now he knew he was wrong. Creeping Jesus and King Bull were as bad, if not worse, than their instructors back in the training depot.

'Three blasts on my whistle,' King Bull went on, his voice now a hushed whisper, heavy with menace, 'and you might as well turn up your toes and snuff it. And you know why?' he hissed threateningly. 'I'll tell yer. Because I'll turn any of you piss-pansies who makes me blow it three times - *into a scarlet sow!*'

Suddenly, startlingly, with tremendous speed for such a big man, he picked up the gleaming bone cleaver lying on the table next to him and brought it down with a terrific blow. The table splintered as if it were match-wood and the cleaver buried itself up to the handle, which quivered madly, as if it had a life of its own.

For one long terrible moment King Bull glared at their ashen faces, his huge chest heaving, while the cleaver still trembled beside him. Then he turned to the corporal with the poised notebook. 'Tietze,' he said, his voice quite normal now, 'you're in charge of 'em now. But remember, I'll have my beady eye on them cardboard soldiers for the rest of the shift. Remember, no talking, no singing - and above all no smoking!'

Corporal Tietze tut-tutted, as if someone had just cursed the name of God. 'No talking, no singing, and no smoking, *Herr Oberfeldwebel*,' he echoed dutifully.

King Bull nodded his approval and then without another look at the frightened recruits, he took the half-smoked cigar wedged behind his right ear, struck a match on his huge rump, lit it and puffing away happily, strode away as if he had not a care in the whole wide world.

Thus, as the first Christmas of the war approached and in far away Berlin, they planned feverishly for the great offensive to come in the West, the Rebels and their comrades of the Draft learned how to soldier with the illustrious Fourth Grenadier Regiment.

Each morning at four, they rose to wash and shave in icy

cold water before doubling in the winter gloom to the blacked-out cookhouse. With frozen fingers that felt like clumsy sausages, they fumbled and lit the great boilers, which heated the water for the cook's coffee, or 'nigger-sweat', as they called the ersatz stuff contemptuously. Only King Bull, *naturally*, drank coffee made from real beans.

At six the cooks, washed and shaved in the hot water they had prepared, deigned to make their appearance to breakfast off slices of choice sausage and fresh cheese, together with plenty of new bread straight from the regimental bakery, before issuing the fatigue men their orders, which started the real work of the day. And back-breaking enough it was, too. Stirring huge boilers full of turgid porridge for the men's breakfasts; slicing tremendous mounds of bread to make the sandwiches the soldiers who manned the nearby bunkers of the *Westwall** would take with them; lugging great steel buckets of thin 'nigger sweat' to the trestle tables where the Grenadiers waited with their white china bowls for the unappetizing drink.

At eight King Bull himself would appear, twirling that dreaded whistle of his, and even the veterans of the Polish Campaign would gulp down the rest of their watery coffee at the sight of the huge head cook and flee into the cold morning. Now the work of the harassed, wretched fatigue men would intensify as the abruptly alert, brisk and industrious cooks began piling up huge stacks of dirty dishes, clogged cutlery, and scummed pans in front of them at the littered, stinking washing-up benches.

There, under King Bull's suspicious gaze, as he swaggered back and forth, swinging his damned whistle and smoking one of his cheap black cigars, they laboured mightily, fatigues black with sweat, wreathed in steam, hands grey and wrinkled from being immersed in hot water constantly, looking as if they had been infected by some loathsome skin disease. At night they were too exhausted even to attempt to

*The great fortified line running the length of Nazi Germany's frontier, called in the UK/USA 'the Siegfried Line'.

sample the meagre pleasures of the medieval Swabian villages that dotted the plain of the Rhine around the *Adolf Hitler Kaserne*. Instead, unwashed and unshaven, they tumbled into their freezing bunks and fell asleep at once to be awakened almost immediately (or so it seemed to the harassed young men) by the rattle of the orderly corporal's stick along the line of rickety wooden bunks and that harsh unfeeling voice crying: '*Aufstehen* . . . Hands off yer cocks and on with yer socks . . . Come on now, you bunch of asparagus Tarzans . . . *AUFSTEHEN*!' And yet another endless day of backbreaking, unrelenting labour in King Bull's kitchen would commence . . .

'It ain't frigging fair!' Ami, the smallest of the three Rebels, complained more than once that first long week with the Fourth Grenadiers. 'I didn't join the frigging army to wash up for the whole of the frigging *Wehrmacht*. Will yer cast yer glassy orbits on my hands.' And he would hold up his wrinkled little fingers which looked as if they were being attacked by a severe case of leprosy, for their inspection. 'Them fingers,' he would moan plaintively, 'is meant for loving-up beautiful women, dipping in that delightful juicy honey-pot they've got between their legs, *not* for frigging pearl-diving in that muck!' And he would indicate the sink, filled to the top with greasy, scummy water in which floated the disgusting remains of the previous meal.

Polack's reaction was invariably to hawk and spit into whatever special meal was being prepared at the time for King Bull; while Karl would wipe the sweat from his forehead with the back of his dripping hand and console his two comrades, with: 'Just stick it out fellers, it won't be long now before we can kiss goodbye to the big bastard!'

But the manner of their leaving from the 'big bastard's' kitchen was more startling - and would be sooner - than the three young friends expected.

On Friday December 18th, 1939, it was announced that the Regiment, apart from the men manning the *Westwall* bunkers along the Rhine, would be stood down for three days over Christmas. The Führer, with his infinite kindness and well-known love for his fellow men, had also ordered that all frontline units would receive extra rations for the Christmas Eve festivities.

'Frigging pork chops, red cabbage and fried potatoes, plus one litre of beer per man *per-haps*,' King Bull announced scornfully to the assembled kitchen staff, reading out the regimental order. 'What's the frigging *Wehrmacht* coming to? You'd think this was a frigging home for frigging retired gentlewomen! *Pork chops, indeed!*' He had stuffed the order angrily into his pocket and stalked off, face purple with rage at such decadent softness.

The three Rebels could hardly contain their joy. Even Polack, afflicted as he was occasionally by Slavic gloom, remarked, 'Just imagine it, comrades, three days in bed, our guts filled with pork chops and red cabbage!'

Ami's wicked dark eyes glittered at the thought. 'Get me a piece o' that pork inside me guts, and perhaps I'll get a blue-veiner again.' He clutched his crotch dramatically. 'I ain't had a frigging diamond cutter ever since I came to this frigging place!'

Perhaps it was the general euphoria of that snowy Friday, with the knowledge that they had only one more day to serve in King Bull's kitchens and that soon they would have three whole days of rest, that did it, making the three Rebels so careless. But some two hours after the midday meal composed of what the cooks called 'fart-soup' and 'old man' (pea soup with slices of salt beef reputedly made of the bodies of old men from Berlin's workhouses), the three Rebels collapsed behind a huge stack of washing up and allowed themselves a quick smoke. Happily they slumped there in their greasy fatigues, watching the snowflakes drift down slowly above the fanlight, savouring their cigarettes, too weary even to talk.

It was thus that Creeping Jesus surprised them in the very same instant that King Bull spotted the blue cigarette smoke rising from the piled-high table and was tugging out his celebrated whistle to blow the feared three blasts, prior to making 'scarlet sows' of the unknown criminals.

'What piggery is this!' Creeping Jesus cried. 'What terrible abomination . . . in, in,' he stuttered with rage, the monocle popping out of his eye with the effort, 'in the mess of the . . . Fourth Grenadier Regiment . . . *Smoking*!'

As one they sprang to their feet, Ami trying to swallow his cigarette, Karl dropping his to the floor as if it were red-hot; while Polack was so surprised that he could do nothing but continue smoking, exuding twin jets of blue smoke from his big nostrils.

For what seemed an eternity the officer stared at the culprits, while King Bull towered behind him, his face scarlet with anger, fists clenched in impotent rage, as his piglike eyes threatened some awesome fate to these criminals who had abused the sanctity of his kitchens so fiendishly. Finally Creeping Jesus made up his mind what to do with the sullen young men facing him. 'There will be no Christmas break for you lot of rogues,' he announced. 'You will stop fatigues at once and report to the orderly sergeant immediately – in full field marching order!'

Karl swallowed hard, while Polack finally managed to overcome his shock and stop smoking. 'May I be so bold as to ask, sir,' he ventured cautiously, 'where we will be going, sir?'

Creeping Jesus smirked maliciously. 'You may be so bold, soldier,' he answered. 'I will order the orderly sergeant to send you into the line in the next truck. Christmas 1939, you will be *celebrating*, if that's the right word for it, in a freezing bunker of the *Westwall*. Now off you go – at the double!'

They fled, glad to escape the kitchen while the officer was still there to save them from the wrath of an enraged King Bull, who threatened to explode at any moment . . .

CHAPTER 3

KARL WATCHED, half amused, half apprehensive, as the elderly corporal with his drooping, tea-strainer moustache, prepared for the patrol. Standing there in the comfortable fug of the bunker, Corporal Thoma tugged an old scarf across his skinny chest, tying it like a schoolkid's behind his back with a safety pin. Now came the newspaper stuffed into his tunic, followed by the earmuffs. Finally he slipped into what he called his 'spook suit', a crude white camouflage jacket made of an old sheet, probably stolen from the quartermaster's stores.

He beamed at Karl and took another puff at the little clay pipe which never seemed to leave his mouth, and said, 'You might laugh, Grenadier Carstens, but it's cold enough to freeze up yer outside plumbing down there by the Rhine. A man's got to dress hissen up warm, especially if he's delicate like me.' He coughed hollowly, as if to emphasize his point.

Karl grinned and heaved his rifle onto his shoulder. He liked the corporal. Veteran as he was of the recent Polish Campaign and service in the trenches in the First War, Corporal Thoma did just enough to keep himself out of trouble. Otherwise his main concern was to keep the little bunker under his command warm and ensure that he had a plentiful supply of shag for his beloved pipe.

Thoma took a final look around the bunker, with its six bunks and pot-bellied stove glowing a dull scarlet in the corner, the gun slits in the walls plugged up with rags (against regulations) to keep out the icy December wind, and apparently liked what he saw. He, too, slung his rifle and, shifting his pipe from one corner of his mouth to the other, said to Polack, 'You, Grenadier Zimanski, you're in charge. If you hear footsteps outside, pull them rags out of the slits and pretend as if you're about to repel the whole of the frigging frog army.'

'But what if a frog patrol *does* come this way, Corporal?' Ami, who was lounging on the bunk nearest the glowing stove, asked a little anxiously.

Corporal Thoma shook his old head as if in wonder at the foolishness of youth. 'You ought to know better than that, Grenadier Doepgen. Holy strawsack, a frog patrol in weather like this! Yer average frog's got his head screwed on the right way. He's tucked away safely in his bunker, with his sun-ray lamps and his wine, probably scoffing frogs' legs or snails or something. Only yer frigging stupid German Army sends a man on patrol in this kind o' weather!' He spat a stream of deep-brown tobacco juice onto the floor contemptuously. 'All right, Grenadier Carstens, you've got yer party frock on, so we'd better be off to the frigging dance. And remember this, keep yer turnip and yer ass down out there, just in case some frog, who's feeling a bit liverish, takes a pot shot at us. *Gut*. Grenadier Zimanski, look after the shop. We're off.' He pushed aside the gas curtain that covered the rear exit to the little bunker and stepped out.

Karl winked with more confidence than he felt at Polack and Ami and followed.

Outside a murderous wind blew across the snow-bound plain of the Rhine straight from Siberia. Karl blinked and gasped and wished for a moment he had followed the old corporal's example and put on every piece of spare clothing he possessed, but it was too late for that now. So, he hitched his rifle more comfortably on his shoulder and plodded through the ankle-deep snow after the old man.

They might have been alone in that desolate winter world. The countryside, as far as the eye could see, all appeared to be deserted. No smoke rose from the chimneys of the little village to their front. Even the birds had abandoned the skeletal trees. But Karl knew the apparently empty plain was deceptive. The village was one of the *Westwall's* strongpoints. Those seemingly tumbledown medieval houses were really made of reinforced concrete and were manned by a whole battalion of infantry. Behind them, each of those snow-covered mounds on the heights was in reality a gunpit, housing long-range cannon capable of firing deep into the heart of French Alsace on the other side of the River Rhine.

Corporal Thoma seemed to read Karl's thoughts, for he paused for a moment and said, working his pipe from one side of this mouth to the other, 'Daft, isn't it, when yer come to think on it? Thousands of German soldiers burrowed deep in the earth all around us and on the other side of the Rhine, thousands of frogs, too, and all of 'em playing games like frigging kids!' Again he spat contemptuously. They plodded on.

Ten minutes later they breasted a slight rise and Karl caught his first glimpse of the great river which separated France and Germany and which was going to play such a dramatic role soon in the history of the Fourth Grenadier Regiment. Now Corporal Thoma was suddenly businesslike and alert. He stuffed his pipe into the pocket of his white 'spook suit' and snapped urgently, 'All right, Carstens, this is where the wet fart can hit the side of the thunderbox. Left of that pine at three o'clock, just above the bank there, that's where the frogs have got their first observation post – only five hundred metres away – and if they ain't stuffing their frog necks full of snails or whatever other disgusting shit they call grub over there, they'll have already spotted us. So watch it. Come on!' Moving quickly now, hugging what little cover there was, bodies crouched low and tense, ears alert for the first dry crack of a rifle, the two lone figures hurried towards their own observation post: a small wooden stand of the kind used by hunters before the war, camouflaged by white-painted sheets of metal.

'Have a dekko now,' Thoma said, stepping back from the telescope set on the wooden platform, its lens peering through a slit in the sheet of metal. 'To left and right of what's left of the bridge, you'll see the first of their pillboxes, guarding the road. Then if you follow the road towards the village on the horizon – the place is named Gambsheim by the way – you'll see Fort de Gambsheim, that's the frogs' main stronghold on the road between Strasbourg and Hagenau.'

THE FIRST CLASH, GAMBSHEIM DEC 24th, 1939

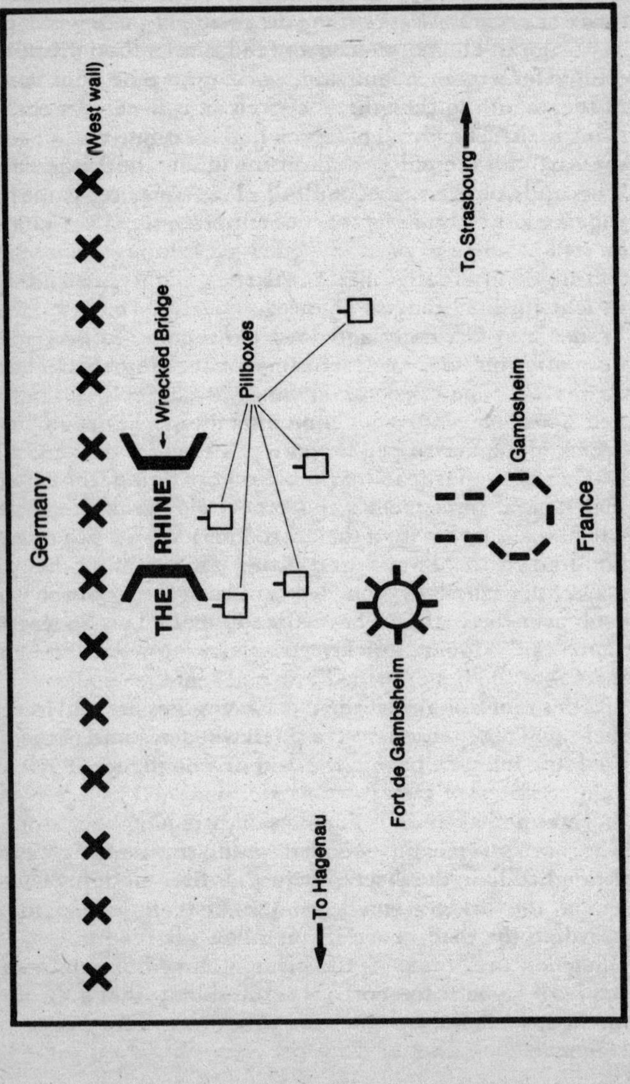

Puzzled a little by the old corporal's knowledge and the confidence with which he detailed the Maginot Line fortifications on the other side of the Rhine, Karl pressed his eye to the telescope. Immediately the opposite bank sprang into view in the centre of the circle of calibrated glass: the remains of the bridge the French had blown up at the start of the war; the twin pillboxes guarding it; and the dead-straight little road, mysteriously cleared of snow, which led to the little village on the horizon. Just as on the German side, there was no sign of life, and no smoke emerged from the chimneys of the half-timbered Alsatian village. Gambsheim too, it appeared, had been abandoned.

Karl frowned. He still had not spotted the fort – what had Thoma called it? 'I can't make out that Fort de – you know, Corporal,' he said, adjusting the lenses.

'Fort de Gambsheim,' Thoma said and grinned. 'I'm not surprised, my lad. Cos most of it is underground. The frogs who man it call themselves *écrevisses* – that's "crabs" to you – because like them they spend most of their time in the depths. But if you look agen, a bit more careful, you'll spot eight mounds spaced out at regular intervals.'

Karl peered down the telescope again. 'Yes, got one – and another,' he cried excitedly, as he spotted the slight bumps in the thick blanket of snow running along the road, 'eight of them in all!'

'That's them,' Thoma said, puffing stolidly at his old pipe, holding his gloved hand above the bowl so that the smoke would not give them away. 'That's all you can see of the fort. Eight retractable gun mounts, each manned by a gun crew and a bunch of infantry to protect them.'

Slowly Karl raised himself from the periscope and stared puzzled at the wrinkled old corporal, who suddenly winked slyly at the young grenadier and said, 'Well, go on, lad, ask me what you're thinking!'

'Well, Corp, I was just thinking – how do you know so much about the other side?' He bit his bottom lip. 'I mean, you talk as if you've been over there, sort of?'

Thoma took his pipe from between his lips and wiped his

moustache dry. 'Not only have I been over there, Grenadier Carstens, but I was *frigging well born over there*!'

Abruptly he was laughing at the look of sheer astonishment on Karl's face as the latter stuttered, 'But you're not a frog – I mean, a Frenchman, are yer, Corp?'

'*Of course, I am*!' was the old man's surprising reply . . .

'You see, it's like this,' Thoma said patiently, after Karl had recovered from his surprise and the two of them squatted down on the little bench on the tower out of the wind, sipping from the flask of cold tea and rum which Thoma had brought with him for their two-hour vigil. 'Alsace over there had changed hands a dozen times in its history until 1870 when the Prussians took it off the frogs, and they kept it until the frogs took it back after we lost the war in 1918.'

Karl nodded. 'Yes, now I remember my old man told me something about it. Versailles, wasn't it, the Treaty of Versailles?'

'That's right. Now the people over there have always spoken German as their main language, but while the Prussians ruled they brought in thousands of German emigrants from Prussia and Bavaria, who after 1918 automatically became frog like I did.' He chuckled softly. 'Half the frogs in those bunkers on the other side at this very moment will probably be of German extraction, with not a single drop of frog blood in their veins. Funny, ain't it?' He laughed hollowly and took a drag at his pipe.

Karl frowned. Again he was reminded of the folly of war. One day they might have to fight those men over there and kill them, men who could well be related to them. Once more he determined that when that time came, he'd get out of the fighting. The knowledge that there were men of German blood over there was just one more reason for not serving the workers' arch-enemy Adolf Hitler. But he didn't tell Corporal Thoma that. One never knew in National Socialist Germany. Only Polack and Ami, rebels themselves, knew of his intention not to fight. Instead he asked, 'So you lived over there, Corp, then?'

'Yes, number ten *Rue de Strasbourg*, Gambsheim to be exact,' Thoma frowned. 'I have a look at it with the telescope every time I come up here. There I was born and there I had hoped to die - in peace, just as my parents had done and their parents had done before them. But that wasn't to be.'

'What happened?'

'It started when the government in Paris decided to build the Maginot Line, right through Alsace. It was all right at first. All the local men found work digging the foundations, mixing concrete for the bunkers, and that sort of thing. There was plenty of money in Gambsheim and all the rest of the border villages in them days. But then the trouble started, once Paris began to garrison the forts.' He took a puff at his old pipe and made a sour face, as if his tobacco suddenly didn't taste right. 'You see the "crabs", as they are called, went down into the underground forts for fifteen days at a time. You see, lad, it's not like this *Westwall* of ours, all very simple and primitive. The frog forts have got cinemas and hospitals and sun-ray lounges - they even grow their own mushrooms down there!'

Karl was duly impressed.

'But the catch was that we of military age along the border, in spite of the fact that a lot of us had fought for Germany against France in the Old War, were turned into a local militia and we had to go down with the regulars periodically. The idea was that if Germany attacked, the whole line could be fully garrisoned within an hour!'

Karl stared at the old corporal. 'You mean you've actually been down inside that - er - Fort de Gambsheim over there?' he gasped.

'More than frigging once,' the corporal replied gloomily. 'And you can't imagine, lad, what hell it is. The noise is terrific and it's always damp when the concrete sweats. People get depressed and some even try to commit suicide. The frogs call it *betonité*.' He clicked his fingers impatiently. 'What would you call it in German? *Concretitis*, something like that. It's frigging awful, and after a couple o' times, I'd had a right noseful. Right up to here! So I voted with my feet.'

'What?'

'I just crossed the Rhine one morning and started working over here, building our own *Westwall*, and then the trouble started all over again. Our beloved Führer,' he spat contemptuously into the snow, 'invited me to go on a merry little jaunt to Poland where that asshole of a colonel of ours lost over half the regiment. And now I'm here agen, suffering from concretitis on the other side of the Rhine.'

There was silence, broken only by the harsh cawing of the rooks in the black, skeletal trees while Karl pondered the old corporal's strange story. A long, long way away a heavy machine-gun chattered relentlessly, but neither the corporal not Karl seemed to hear it.

Finally Karl said, thinking aloud, 'Then, seeing you know the place, you'd be the ideal man, Corp, to guide our troops if they ever did attack that place over there.'

Thoma shuddered dramatically. 'Don't even frigging *think* things like that, Carstens!' he snorted angrily. 'If I ever get back to good old Gambsheim, I want to do it peacefully. In a civvie suit, with a civvie case in my hand and not a frigging rifle.' He looked at a somewhat surprised Karl, as if he were seeing him for the first time. 'Take the advice of an old hare, Carstens. If yer keep yer ass open and yer trap shut, yer turnip down and yer chin up, you might be lucky and end this frigging war as a civvie.' And with that he lapsed into an angry silence, puffing moodily at his pipe, while an embarrassed Karl decided it would be better for him to be occupied pretending to view the opposite bank with the telescope . . .

But Corporal Jean-Paul Thoma was not fated to return to his home town with that civvie case in his hand. Already the die had been cast. Corporal Thoma would never see number ten, *Rue de Strasbourg* again.

CHAPTER 4

COLONEL VON Heinersdorff waited patiently as his officers began to assemble there in the big conference room. Sitting astride of the horse saddle which was his favourite seat, slapping the broken sword which he had carried at the Battle of Bzura, he acknowledged the salute of each new officer with a gentle nod of his greying head, the usual absent, idiotic smile on his lean old face.

Outside it was snowing heavily and the sentries guarding the conference room for the secret meeting were bowed under a mantel of white, their faces under their helmets blue and miserable. Von Heinersdorff smiled at the sight and told himself cheerfully that a bit of rough weather was good for the men; it would harden them for what was soon to come.

The last officer entered the room, clicked to attention and saluted. Von Heinersdorff beamed in that inane manner of his. It was the adjutant von Schorr, one of the veterans of Bzura. 'A good man to have with you in a scrap,' he told himself. Aloud he said, 'Oh, there you are, Adjutant. Be a good fellow and lock the door. We can start now. But we mustn't have any leaks.' He frowned at the word, as if he had just suddenly become aware that it had another meaning. 'Well you all know what I mean, don't you, gentlemen?'

There was a polite mutter of agreement and von Schorr, turning to lock the door, told himself the old man was ripe for the rubber van and the funny farm. He was very definitely dotty.

Colonel von Heinersdorff sat bolt upright in his saddle and whacked the broken sword against the side of his highly polished riding boots 'Well, gentlemen, you will be exceedingly pleased to know that the balloon will definitely go up in the New Year! I've had it officially from division. The enemy has yet again turned down the Führer's generous offer of peace. So the attack west *will* take place. 1940 will see the Fourth

Grenadier Regiment – the good old Crown Prince's Own – marching into battle once more.' He beamed at his officers idiotically, broken sword suddenly raised, as if he was once again leading that desperate charge at Bzura.

Most of the younger officers who had not taken part in the disastrous Polish campaign exclaimed with delight at the news, suddenly chattering excitedly among themselves. But the few survivors of Bzura remained sombre and silent, their faces set, as if they were pondering the announcement and not liking their conclusions one bit. For his part the adjutant felt a cold finger of fear trace its way down his spine.

'We are back to the original plan,' the Colonel continued. 'The main body of the army will attack through Luxembourg and Belgium in order to outflank the Maginot Line. Our role here on the Upper Rhine remains mostly one of containment. But you will all be delighted to know there has been one *small* change.' He paused and swayed back and forth in the well-polished saddle, as if he were charging once more into those Polish bullets which had decimated his grenadiers, leaving the fields along the river littered with their dead bodies.

The adjutant swallowed hard and waited for the old fool's next words, hoping desperately that they would not mean the Regiment would actually have to fight in this new campaign in the West. But Creeping Jesus was doomed to be disappointed. For the colonel said: 'High Command has ordered we are to create a diversion. In Berlin they don't want any French troops moved out of the Maginot to meet the threat in the north. So, *meine Herren*, I am happy to tell you that the Fourth Grenadiers will have the honour of being the only part of the army on the Upper Rhine which will cross the river to attack an objective on French soil. When the balloon does go up, the Fourth will make an assault crossing of the Rhine and attack Fort de Gambsheim!'

Creeping Jesus felt sick. His legs seemed to turn to water. He caught himself just in time from lurching against the door behind him, he was so weak. 'Does that mean, sir,' he heard himself ask, 'that we are to take part in a feint . . . incurring casualties . . . for no real purpose?' He gulped, mouth suddenly parched, and he could say no more.

'Yes, I suppose you could put it like that, von Schorr. It is a great honour that has been accorded to the Regiment, all the same.' The colonel laughed in that unthinking manner of his and swung the broken sword. 'One can't make an omelette without cracking a few eggs, can one?'

'No sir,' Creeping Jesus heard himself answer faintly, as the colonel continued . . .

That first week of September, the Fourth Grenadiers had marched and marched across Poland. In the blistering heat, they had stalked the Polacks through shoulder-high fields of sunflowers, picking them off easily like game birds on the rise. Before them, the tanks had rumbled and the Stukas had fallen out of the burning sky like deadly metal gulls. The monstrous, mechanized juggernaut, of a kind the world had never seen before, had swept all before it relentlessly, remorsely. This was the Blitzkrieg; the Führer's war-winning tactic. *Nothing could stop it!*

That had been until they had come to that damned river. They had reached it as the blood-red ball of the sun had begun to sink on the burning horizon, flecked by black pillars of smoke reaching high into the sky. On both sides of the white road, the Polacks had been stacked like cord-wood. Dead and dying cavalry horses littered the shelled fields on both sides. The air was filled with the sweet cloying stench of the bloated Polack corpses, blackened in the burning September sun. It was so bad that many of the grenadiers had urinated on their handkerchieves and tied them around their noses and mouths like primitive gas-masks, as they staggered to an exhausted stop before the remains of the bridge wrecked by the retreating Polacks.

The Old Man had not even dismounted from his weary, sweat-lathered horse. 'Adjutant,' he had barked, 'we go straight over. Wade on both sides of the bridge. The Polacks must be given no rest, no opportunity to dig in. To the attack!' And like some damnfool of a 19th century commander in a romantic battle portrait of the time, he had waved his sword as the first of the exhausted grenadiers had begun to stumble into the water.

As if someone had thrown a gigantic power switch, the darkening sky above the Bzura had been torn apart by an awesome flash of ugly red light. For what seemed an age, there was only that great burning flame, turning the upturned faces of the shocked grenadiers into hollowed-out crimson death's-heads.

With startling suddenness the whole weight of that tremendous barrage descended upon them, the shells screaming balefully out of the sky to hit the packed ranks of the grenadiers. An instant later the concealed Polack mortars and machine-guns in the undergrowth of the opposite bank had joined in. Frantically the machine-guns had chattered. Mortars howled. Tracer zipped flatly across the boiling white water, churned to a fury by the shells. Mercilessly the triumphant Polacks had poured a hail of fire into the stalled Germans, as a fantastic pattern of stabs and scarlet-forked jabs of flame erupted.

Grenadiers went down everywhere. By the score they were swept off their feet to disappear into the angry water. The Colonel's horse was shot from beneath him, kneeling in the water, whinnying piteously, blood jetting from it in scarlet arcs in half a dozen places. A bugler attempted to sound 'retreat', but went down, the call unplayed, his face dripping onto his chest like red molten wax. There had seemed no end to the hideous murder and mayhem on that damned river . . .

Still Colonel von Heinersdorff had persisted in the attack. Waving his shattered sword and bleeding from an ugly gash on his forehead, he rallied a badly disorganized First Battalion and led it personally into the assault on the Polack machine-guns on the other side.

Screaming with fear and rage, carried away by the wild unreasoning fury of battle, the young grenadiers had slithered down the bank, littered with the bodies of their comrades, and had gone splashing into the water, whipped and tormented by the merciless Polack fire. They hadn't had a chance. Most of them had been mown down before they had gone twenty metres. Then the survivors were streaming back, throwing away their weapons, their eyes wide and wild with outrage, blundering blindly by the colonel and what officers were left. The adjutant had realized that this was the time to save his own skin before that fool of a CO got him killed in yet another attack. He had drawn his pistol and yelled above the racket to King Bull and his cooks who had suddenly appeared out of the smoke, 'Form a skirmish line to the rear, *Oberfeld*! Stop all stragglers. Let no one get through . . . *To the rear, quickly now*!' And gathering the all too eager cooks together, he had set off to the rear and safety. That had been the last he had seen of that damned river; but for weeks afterwards his dreams had been tormented by the ghostly survivors trailing through them, painfully and in total silence, not even asking for aid for their terrible wounds, like sleep-walkers haunted by some terrible never-ending nightmare. *That day the Fourth Grenadier Regiment had suffered eleven hundred casualties, over one third of its strength, most of them dead . . !*

'So, gentlemen,' the Old Man was saying, waving that same damned sword, with which he had led so many young men to their death that terrible September day, 'till the day the great attack is ordered, we must make every effort to keep our chaps on their toes and the French gentlemen on the other side of the Rhine on edge, what?' He beamed idiotically at them, and waved his sword yet once again.

The young officers who had not been in Poland reacted predictably. Innocent faces flushed and excited by the tremendous news the colonel had just given them, they asked eagerly, 'How do you mean, sir? More training, sir . . ? Patrols? What are you suggesting, sir?' Their enthusiastic questions came from all sides, while the survivors of Bzura stared grimly at the softly falling snow, as if they simply couldn't bear to look any longer at those excited young faces of men who would be dead before many months had passed.

'A patrol,' Colonel von Heinersdorff said so softly that at the back of the room the adjutant had to strain to hear what he was saying. 'A fighting patrol.'

'*Across the Rhine?*' one of the young men blurted out excitedly.

The CO nodded. 'Across the Rhine, yes. You see I have discovered that one of our corporals, a man named Thoma, veteran of the trenches and Poland and all that, is a native of Alsace and actually, one can hardly believe our good fortune, comes from Gambsheim over there. Surely he will know the terrain better than anyone.'

There was a murmur of agreement from the eager ones. Creeping Jesus dug his nails into the palms of his sweating hands till it hurt, as he prayed that the old fool would not ask him, as a veteran of the Polish campaign, to lead his damned stupid 'fighting patrol'.

'We need, gentlemen, in essence, two things,' the colonel continued, 'to leave our calling card, as it were, and make the French jumpy; and at the same time take some prisoners who can give us more information on the present state of the defences at Fort de Gambsheim. And what better time to achieve those two aims than when the French will assume we Germans will be celebrating our most important feast day of the year, one on which undoubtedly we will not undertake any military action?' He paused and smiled, almost as if he were expecting some enthusiast to jump in and state the day before he did.

But no one did, though most of them present could guess what day he had selected for the Regiment's first offensive action in the west. It was as if the thought that they would be killing their fellow human beings on this most holy day in the year for a German had soured their enthusiasm for action.

'*Christmas Eve*,' the colonel said somewhat lamely in the end. 'That should come as quite a surprise to the gentlemen on the other side of the Rhine. Now,' he rose from the saddle and braced to attention, running his gaze along the faces of his young officers, 'I am asking for a volunteer from you young subalterns to go along on this patrol as second-in-command to one of my most experienced officers.' He beamed at the adjutant.

Creeping Jesus's heart sank. Numbly he heard a voice, which he barely recognized as his own, saying, 'I'd like to thank you, sir for this great honour . . .'

Ten minutes later he was locked in the isolation of his own quarters vomiting miserably with unreasoning fear, while outside the snow fell and fell as if it would never stop . . .

CHAPTER 5

EERILY THE night mist writhed over the surface of the Rhine, lurking around the snow-heavy bushes of the bank, curling like a silent grey cat through the firs which covered their approach. In single file, placing their feet down carefully on the frozen snow, the men of the fighting patrol followed Corporal Thoma, each one of them silent and wrapped up in a cocoon of his own thoughts.

The silver night was silent save for the sound of their own breathing and the occasional splash of some fish or other in the water. Yet the very silence of this freezing Christmas Eve was frightening, and Karl, marching behind Polack, had constantly to fight off the temptation to throw a glance behind him to check whether they were being followed; though who might be following them he could not imagine.

'Here we stop,' Thoma hissed. 'Pass it on please, Lieutenant.'

Dutifully the young officer passed on the command, whispering as if the French were only five metres away instead of five hundred, and the men crouched on one knee in the snow, hearts beating excitedly. At the rear of the column, Creeping Jesus, carrying a soldier's rifle so that any French sniper this damnfool patrol might encounter would not immediately spot him as an officer, swallowed hard and peered into the silver night beyond the slow snake of the Rhine. The French side of the river had seemingly gone to sleep for the night. There was no sound. Nothing moved.

A sudden plop. Creeping Jesus nearly jumped out of his skin. '*Freeze*!' Thoma hissed urgently.

The men, the hands gripping the rifles suddenly wet with sweat, tensed. Over the other side of the river a flare soared into the sky and exploded with a soft crack, bathing the area below in an abrupt silver glare.

It seemed to hang there for ever. Karl, crouching with the rest, could hear his heart racing away madly, as if it might well burst out of his rib-cage at any moment. A nerve had begun to tick electrically at the side of his face, completely out of control. He realized he was scared.

In front of him, Polack sighed with relief and then cursed in Polish, big hands gripping his rifle as if it was a kid's toy. 'What's the matter?' Karl hissed as Thoma signalled they should get to their feet again.

'It's not right,' Polack hissed angrily, 'not right at all, going out to kill on such a night. No good will come of it, mark my words. No good at all!'

'Stop that talking back there,' Thoma commanded. 'Like a bunch of frigging schoolgirls on a frigging outing!'

At the back of the column Creeping Jesus knew he should reprimand the corporal on account of his language, but he knew, too, everything depended on the grizzled NCO. He decided it was wiser to remain silent.

Now they started moving again down to the frozen reeds, where they had concealed the little rubber and canvas assault boats the night before. By means of sign language, Thoma, muffled up the ears as usual, his thick body draped in his 'spook suit', allotted them to the two boats, placing one officer in each. Thus it was that the three Rebels found themselves in close proximity to Creeping Jesus, wrinkling their noses in contempt at the odour of perfume - and fear - which came from him.

Cautiously, very cautiously, hardly daring to breathe now, they paddled across the great river, any sound they made muffled by the cold wet mist which clung to the surface of the water. All the same, every one of the young soldiers was tense with apprehension. If the frogs spotted them now, they would be sitting ducks. Unable to defend themselves, they were a machine-gunner's dream. It would be a massacre.

Only Thoma, the veteran of the trenches in the Old War, seemed completely unconcerned. While the others paddled, he took out his top set, examined them seriously in the cold light of the moon, gave the false teeth a rub on the sleeve of his 'spook suit' and then, apparently satisfied, replaced them.

Now they were only a matter of metres away from the

French side. They narrowed their eyes to slits and peered at the bank. It was empty. All they could see was patches of rusting barbed wire among the reeds, placed there years before. 'Stop paddling,' Thoma commanded softly. 'Let the current carry us the rest of the way.'

They stopped immediately and tensed as the little boats hurried towards the frozen reeds, each man's body poised for the first red-hot impact of enemy fire.

None came. A moment later the first of the Grenadiers was cracking through the frozen reeds, cursing as they caught their uniforms on the barbed wire, making a noise, a quaking Creeping Jesus told himself, that must surely wake up the dead. But the dead slept on and a few moments later Creeping Jesus found himself on French soil for the first time. The first stage of the patrol had been completed . . .

It was the singing which alerted them first to their danger. As they stole down the road which led to Gambsheim, strung out on both sides, weapons at the ready, it came to them, frightening yet somehow familiar, as the chant was carried to them by the faint breeze.

Thoma held up his hand for them to halt and then hissed in wonder, 'Great crap on the Christmas tree – it's "*Stille Nacht, Heilige Nacht!*"'*

The young lieutenant's mouth dropped open foolishly and he said, 'But they're singing in German!'

'Of course, they're frigging Alsatians!' Thoma controlled his anger in time and hissed, 'We've got to locate them – *fast*!'

Behind him, Ami whispered in awe to Karl, 'We can't nobble our own folk, can we, Karl?'

Karl bit his bottom lip and didn't reply, but Polack growled angrily, 'This heathen lot'd croak their own granny. I knew nothing would come of it. *Boshe moi*, fighting on Christmas Eve . . . heathen it is . . .'

**Silent Night.*

'*There*, Lieutenant!' Thoma whispered urgently. 'To the right of that clump of firs. You can just see the chink of light coming from the barn. Franz Deutscherle used it as a tobacco barn in the old days. The frog troops are obviously using it now.'

Creeping Jesus pushed his way to the head of the column. 'What's all this chat?' he demanded angrily, knowing that every minute they spent on French territory might cost him his precious life. 'In three devils' name let's get on with it and get back to the damned boats!'

But they're singing in German sir,' the young lieutenant objected. 'They're our own people in a way, I suppose,' he added lamely.

'If they're in the French Army, they're the enemy, *Herr Leutnant*,' Creeping Jesus snapped severely, 'and don't you forget it. Damned border pack! Now send your men up there and find your prisoners. The rest, under my command, will cover your line of withdrawal, *Klar, Herr Leutnant?*'

'Clear, sir!' the lieutenant answered and hastily indicated that Corporal Thoma's section should follow him. A moment later they had disappeared into the silver gloom . . .

'Would you let me do it, sir?' Thoma asked, as they crouched there some twenty metres from the dark outline of the old tobacco barn, listening to the singing and the talk in the harsh Alemanic dialect of Alsace. 'I speak the language in a way.' He looked pleadingly at the young officer.

The Lieutenant bit his lip, torn between duty and the knowledge that the unseen soldiers were just as much German as he was, in spite of the fact that they wore the uniform of the enemy. 'All right, Corporal,' he said in the end. 'But for God's sake, don't build any shit, or Captain von Schorr'll saw my ass off!'

Thoma grinned. 'Don't worry, sir. We'll get our prisoners without a shot being fired. You three,' he beckoned to the Rebels, 'follow me and keep your cakeholes shut. But take off them helmets first.' Without waiting for them to do so,

Thoma removed his own helmet and carefully placed it down. 'Right, pick up yer hindlegs and move.'

Obediently, their hearts racing madly, the three young men 'picked up their hindlegs' and followed old Thoma, who was now walking quite openly towards the barn, his rifle pressed to his side so that it looked as if he were using a crutch.

Suddenly, surprisingly, when they had almost reached the place, Thoma began to sing in dialect. For one moment Karl, his nerves tingling with the shock, thought Thoma had gone off his head. Then he realized what the old NCO was up to and he grinned. The old fox knew exactly what he was doing.

'*Halt! Wer da?*' The challenge came in German, but it was easy and relaxed. A dark figure, muffled in a heavy overcoat and helmet, detached itself from the shadow cast by the barn, rifle at the ready.

Corporal Thoma stopped and swayed, as if he might well be drunk. '*Abend, Kamerad*,' he said in the local dialect, slurring his words. 'Got anything to drink left inside there –' His right arm shot out and the sentry reeled back abruptly, rifle tumbling to the snow, clutching at his eyes as the black pepper exploded in them. Thoma smashed the cruelly shod butt of his rifle into the sentry's belly and he went down, gasping like a suddenly deflated balloon. An instant later Polack pole-axed him with one blow from his mighty fist and they were grouped at the door, tensed and panting, as if they had just run a race, ready to move in.

Silently Thoma called off the seconds, Suddenly he hissed '*Three*' and with a quick jerk of his wrist opened the barn door. It was packed with men, faces red with drink, as they lolled at rough wooden farm benches, awash with beer and wine, the cigar smoke as thick as the fog outside. Some were already 'beer corpses', sprawled on the straw-covered floor or slumped with their heads in pools of beer, mugs clutched in nerveless fingers. Others were well on their way to that delightful state; while a few still stolidly chewed on the special ration of Strasbourg goose and the local *tarte flambee** issued

*'Flamed tart', a local speciality made with onions.

for the most important day in the Alsatian calendar.

For what seemed an eternity, the two groups simply stared at each other in bewilderment, the Germans panting with red-faced excitement, but unable for some strange reason to move; the French soldiers, mouths filled with food or with mugs poised at their lips, gaping at the intruders, as if they might well just have landed from Mars.

Corporal Thoma moved first. 'All right,' he said in his Alsatian German. 'There is no need for trouble, if you do as you're told. All of you rise to your feet and put your hands above your heads. I promise no harm will come to you . . . After all, I'm from Gambsheim myself. Now - *move it*!'

Stunned, faces registering complete bewilderment, the Frenchmen began to kick back their benches and rise in the same instant that the young lieutenant shot through the door to come to a sudden halt. 'Great balls of fire!' he exclaimed in wonder, 'Corporal, you must have captured the whole frigging French army!' He gulped and gasped. 'There must be at least fifty of them . . . What in the name of God are we going to do with them all?'

One moment later that particular problem was solved for him. Up in the gallery, a young officer, complete with the jaunty *kepi* of the French Infantry appeared suddenly, brandishing a pistol. Even as Corporal Thoma raised his rifle, the Frenchman cried to the bemused Alsatians, '*Sales cons . . . ils sonts les boches . . .*' and fired.

The young lieutenant standing next to Karl reeled back, a sudden hole drilled in the centre of his forehead . . .

CHAPTER 6

THE BURST of automatic fire ripped the length of the door. Sparks and slivers of wood flew everywhere. Ami yelped with pain and let his rifle fall to the cobbles with a clatter, crying, 'Karl, the pig-fuckers've gone and shot me in the arm!'

Next to him Polack fired from the hip, as the French soldiers raced to the closed door. Inside there were shrieks and screams. Blood spurted from the holes, bright red in the silver light of the moon.

Karl grabbed a moaning, shocked Ami and cried, 'Come on, run for Chrissake!' in the same instant that Thoma yelled, 'Forget the looey, he's snuffed it . . . Back down the road . . . *Back to the frigging boats. They're on to us!*'

Desperately the little group of Germans began to fall back down the road they had come, as flares hissed into the night sky and tracer started to zip towards them from the barn like flights of angry red hornets. Bugles sounded the alarm. Whistles shrilled. Officers shouted angry orders and Karl told himself, with a sinking feeling, the whole of the fucking Maginot Line was being alerted!

Now they were backing off down the road they had come, firing and running, ducking as bursts of fire came their way, waiting for that first flare to explode above them and give them away. Already there was the angry snap-and-crackle of small-arms fire to the front, between them and the Rhine, and Corporal Thoma shouted angrily, 'The frogs have bumped into Creeping Jesus's lot!'

'What we gonna do, Corp?' Ami asked, his arm stuck in his tunic now in a sort of makeshift sling, while Polack carried his rifle.

'Get off this frigging road for a start,' Thoma gasped. '*Los!*' After me –'

A dark figure sprang from the ditch to his right and Thoma shot him without even aiming. The Frenchman reeled, hands clutched to his destroyed face like a hysterical woman.

Karl gasped with the horror of it all. Men being killed as easily as snapping one's fingers. But this was not the time or place for finer thoughts. Now it was going to be – kill or be killed. Instinctively he knew the enraged French would take no prisoners this night. He sprang over the writhing moaning body of the Frenchman dying in the ditch and floundered after the others through the deep snow . . .

They crouched in the frozen reeds, trembling with the cold and gasping frantically for breath, as to their rear the darkness continued to be stabbed by angry red flashes and they could hear the enraged shouts of men fighting and dying. Who they were back there they didn't know – Creeping Jesus's party or those who had been left behind from their own in their headlong flight across the snow – and most of them didn't care: they were too concerned about saving their own skins.

'All right,' Thoma swallowed hard and fought to control his breathing, 'this is what we're gonna do. There's not a chance in hell that we'll be able to get back to the boats. Nor can we find a boat along the river bank. The frogs will have collected them all up at the beginning of the war, that's for sure.'

He let his words sink in, as back on the road someone moaned piteously, as if he were dying; a sound so eerie and mournful that it made Karl shiver.

'So we've got to make our own boat.'

'How we gonna do *that*?' Polack growled dourly, his heavy Slavic face set and glum in the silver light. 'We ain't even got a frigging hammer.' He spat contemptuously into the snow.

Thoma shook his old head. 'Grenadier Zimanski, you're a right little bundle o' joy, ain't yer? I bet you really enjoy making people happy.'

Polack mumbled something and hung his head, as if he were suddenly ashamed.

'Of course we can't build our own boat,' Thoma went on,

'but we can make one. You see a bit further down the bank there's an abandoned barn. Now if we're lucky, we can nip off part of the wall – they're all made of planks hereabouts – and make a makeshift raft. It's better than swimming, believe you me . . .'

Captain von Schorr felt the same at exactly that moment, but he knew he had no other choice. Five minutes before he had abandoned the rest of his men to their fate, thrown away his rifle, and run off into the darkness. Now he knew he had only minutes before the French dealt with the trapped soldiers and came down to search the river bank for survivors. He made up his mind. Swiftly he pulled off his boots. His tunic followed. Now he tried the water, already shivering uncontrollably with the bone-chilling cold. He gasped with shock. It was as if he had just placed his foot inside King Bull's storage room. The water was like burning ice. He hesitated, for the river seemed immense. How could he swim it at such a temperature? But not for long.

'Help me, for God's sake, help me, sir?' A gory figure staggered out the gloom, one hand held in front like that of a blind man feeling his way, the other clasped to the empty socket of his right eye. 'Please, don't let them get me, sir . . .' The man staggered and fell to one knee, sobbing piteously, the blood streaming down his young face. Creeping Jesus hesitated no longer. The man's sobs would attract the French. Steeling himself for what was to come, he started to wade into the icy water, gasping with the shock of it; while behind him the blinded soldier slumped helplessly into the snow, sobbing as if his very heart was broken . . .

Karl, leading the little group of survivors along the river bank, bumped into the French soldier completely unexpectedly. One moment the path ahead was empty; the next the Frenchman had appeared from the frozen reeds and was standing there, barring the way. '*Que fait* –'

Karl acted instinctively, as the others blundered to a stop behind him. The big Frenchman's query ended in a yelp of pain as Karl lashed out with his boot and caught the Frenchman a savage blow on the right shin. He staggered backwards and Karl dived forward, knowing that if he used his weapon he would alert the enemy. In a confused heap of flailing arms and legs, they crashed down the embankment, the frozen reeds crackling and snapping under them like fireworks, and tumbled into the icy water.

Both gasped with shock. For a moment they simply lay there, clasped in each other's arms like satiated lovers. Karl then brought up his elbow to smash into the Frenchman's nose and silence him. But the other man was quicker. He grabbed hold of Karl's genitals and twisted hard.

A sickening wave of pain swept though Karl's body. Vomit flooded his throat and drowned the scream of absolute agony which had welled up from deep inside him. Desperately he jabbed at the Frenchman's contorted face with his elbow. Something snapped audibly. Thick gobs of blood splattered the snow. His vicelike grip on Karl's genitals weakened a little.

But Karl knew he couldn't last much longer. Red and silver stars were exploding before his eyes. A great roaring that threatened to overcome him at any moment had commenced. He was going to black out!

Frantically he grabbed for the Frenchman's helmet strap. He found it and tugged hard, pulling the helmet from his cropped head and forcing the strap into his neck. The Frenchman choked. He wriggled and writhed, trying to break that murderous stranglehold. His grip on Karl slackened and than gave altogether. Still Karl held on. The Frenchman slapped the water desperately with his hand, like a wrestler signalling a submission; that he was beaten. But Karl wouldn't let go – *couldn't*! He was carried away by some dark primeval fury. He tugged and tugged. The Frenchman's struggles grew ever weaker. Strange meaningless sounds were coming from within his tortured body. Blood jetted from his ears. Still Karl held on, exerting all his strength. The Frenchman's spine arched as tight as a bowstring in one last desperate attempt to break free. Sobbing for breath, his face glazed with sweat, Karl fought to retain his hold. Abruptly the Frenchman went limp. He slapped into the icy water, taking Karl with him.

For what seemed an age Karl lay on top of the dead man, his shoulders heaving with stifled, choking sobs, as he vomited onto the man he had just killed, the tears streaming down his ashen face with passionate abandon. And then Thoma was tugging at his shoulder urgently, hissing, 'Come on, young Karl Carstens . . . Forget it . . . come on'

Karl stared up at him, his eyes wild and bulging, 'But I've just killed . . . a man,' he sobbed, on the verge of hysterics. 'Killed . . . someone, Corp . . . Honest, I didn't want to do it.' His chest heaved and he was racked again by a sudden retching, the tears streaming down his tortured face unheeded.

Thoma stared at the sobbing boy glumly and said, his voice flat and without expression, 'It's war, lad . . . You'll kill more and you won't even think about it . . . Now, come on, let's get on. There isn't much more time left.'

Blindly Karl followed the corporal up the embankment and they trudged on along the path. Behind them, slumped in the water like a broken toy, the unknown Frenchman began to stiffen in the freezing cold.

His teeth chattering crazily in spite of the blankets and the scalding hot tea and rum, the men manning the bunker had forced down him as soon as they had stripped him of his soaked uniform, von Schorr still lied glibly, as he held the phone in a hand that was blue with cold. 'The action was a direct result of Lieutenant Heinz disobeying my orders,' he told the colonel at the other end. 'His men must have panicked. Corporal Thoma, too, must have lost his head.' He took another sip of the tea the soldier offered him, his eyes big with wonder in the yellow light cast by the single bulb in the centre of the bunker. 'What was there left for me to do – but make a fighting retreat? I can say, with all modesty, sir, that we made the enemy pay for their gains.'

'Excellent, von Schorr, excellent,' the colonel muttered gruffly at the other end. 'In the best tradition of the Fourth Grenadiers. And,' he hesitated, 'were there many more casualties?'

Von Schorr said a quick prayer and hoped his lie would never be revealed. 'I'm afraid to report, sir, that I think I'm the sole survivor. Somehow or other in the course of the fighting I found myself in the water . . . then I was simply swimming for my life. And that was that, sir. I didn't see any more of our chaps. I'm sorry sir.'

'Brave fellow,' the Colonel at the other end said hoarsely, and von Schorr could just imagine the old fool at that moment, his eyes filled with tears as he thought of his dead grenadiers. 'I shall recommend you for the Iron Cross, first class, of course.'

'It's my poor chaps who deserve the award, sir,' von Schorr replied stoutly.

'Well said, von Schorr! But now I must let you get some rest after your ordeal. I'll bid you good night and of course, let me wish you a Happy Christmas.' The colonel broke off, as if he were too overcome by emotion to say more.

Von Schorr's face contorted with contempt. What a silly old fool the colonel was. Aloud he said, 'Thank you, sir,' and gave the field phone back to the waiting soldier.

For a while longer he sipped his tea and rum, and pondered his good fortune. It had all turned out well in the end, after all. He had survived Poland; he had survived his first action in the west. Now he knew he would survive the great battle to come in France. He grinned suddenly and told himself he would survive the war, too. 'I'm lucky,' he whispered, while the soldiers stared at him, as if his experiences this night had turned him mad. 'I'm a born survivor.'

Five minutes later he was tucked up in one of the soldiers' bunks, snoring softly, as if he didn't have a care in the world.

CHAPTER 7

'DO YOU know it's frigging Christmas day?' Ami said wearily, as the others used the butts of their rifles to propel the makeshift raft through the water. 'Heaven, arse and cloud-burst,' he exclaimed in a sudden outburst of rage, 'this time last year, I was a civvie in a nice warm bed, humping fat Gerda, the burgomaster's daughter. Going at it like a fiddler's elbow!'

None of the survivors had the strength to comment. Doggedly they continued their paddling, their weary bodies wreathed in the cold mist that lay over the Rhine. Behind them now, the firing had ceased. All was silent on the French side. Instinctively they knew that the rest of the patrol was dead or captured. The Fourth Grenadiers' first action in the west had been a complete disaster.

'And she paid for it afterwards,' Ami continued, his rage vanished as abruptly as it had come. 'Honest she did! Gave me a case of wine, best quality, too. And now I'm spending this Christmas freezing cold in the middle of frigging nowhere, with a hole in my arm. Shit, what a life!'

Thoma breathed hard and said, 'You could be dead, lad, like those other poor buggers.' He dipped his rifle into the water again wearily.

'Yes,' Karl agreed angrily, 'what was it all for?' He thought of the man he had killed and his anger intensified. 'But by Christ, they're not gonna get me on one of those larks any more! I've had a noseful of this sort of thing.'

Next to him Polack nodded his cropped head in agreement.

Corporal Thoma laughed hollowly. 'Young Carstens, you can't take on the whole of the German Army. Talk like that and one day you'll be ending up in Torgau* – or worse.'

'They've got to catch me first, Corp,' Karl answered, grimly. 'There are ways and means –'

*Notorious military prison.

'Knock it off, Carstens!' Thoma snapped. Look, I think we're almost there . . . through that gap in the fog. It's our bank.'

'By Christ, you're right, Corp,' Ami cried joyously. 'We're almost frigging home!'

Now the weary grenadiers redoubled their efforts, propelling the clumsy raft forward with new energy, all of them animated by the thought of hot drinks and warm beds, relief at last from the bone-chilling cold.

Karl's rifle-butt hit the bottom and he cried, 'We're there, Corp!' Without waiting for an order from Thoma, he slipped over the side, hardly noticing how freezingly cold the water was, and clambered a little up the bank. 'Come on, Ami,' he called. 'Get your digit outa yer orifice and gimme yer flipper.'

Dutifully the wounded Ami reached out his 'flipper' and Karl tugged up his comrade, while Corporal Thoma, good NCO that he was, steadied the raft.

The glare of the searchlight caught them completely by surprise. Already most of the survivors had scrambled up the frozen bank when the bar of hard white light from the other side of the Rhine slammed startingly across the water and blinded them. '*Hit the dirt*!' Thoma shrieked frantically.

Too late! The machine-gun opened up immediately. White tracer zipped across the surface of the water. Corporal Thoma screamed. His arms flailed the air, as if he were climbing the rungs of an invisible ladder, sudden red buttonholes stitched the length of his 'spook suit'. Next instant he fell face forwards into the water, as Polack knelt, ignoring the lead cutting the air all around him, and took aim, deliberately. He grunted and fired. There was a tinkle of glass breaking and the light vanished as suddenly as it had appeared, leaving them crouching there, blinking in the sudden darkness, nerves tingling electrically, as the machine-gun fire died away to leave behind a loud-echoing silence broken only by Corporal Thoma's choking strangling moans.

*

In the light of Polack's torch, protected from the French side by the snow-heavy firs, they peered down at Corporal Thoma. They had slapped their field dressings swiftly over the wounds in his skinny chest and had succeeded in stopping the bleeding, but still Thoma tossed and writhed, his wrinkled old face livid and lathered in sweat as he gasped fervently for breath.

Hesitantly Karl took the corporal's tongue and tried to pull it straight. It didn't help. The semi-conscious soldier still choked. 'I had a kid brother who got diphtheria once,' Ami ventured hesitantly. 'He choked like that and the sawbones saved him by cutting his throat.'

Karl looked up at his friend in horror. '*What?*'

'Well, not really his throat, his wind-pipe so he could breathe.' Ami gulped. 'It saved my kid brother, Karl . . . perhaps you can do it for the corp?'

Karl stared at the faces looking down on him in the yellow light of the torch in horror. '*Me*?' he exclaimed. 'But I wouldn't know –' He broke off and looked again at Thoma.

His breathing was terrible now. Thin and irregular. The neck veins were thick and black with blood. Thoma's face was beginning to turn the same colour as he sobbed and fought for breath, skinny body racked with the effort. The corporal was dying before their eyes. He knew they wouldn't get him to the nearest *Westwall* bunker alive. Thoma would die in the next few minutes if he didn't get air. 'Polack,' Karl cried desperately, 'for Chrissake, hand me yer bayonet!'

Swiftly Polack unsheathed his bayonet, which for reasons known only to himself, he kept honed and razor-sharp. The other rebels had often teased him about it. Wordlessly he handed it to Karl. Karl took it and carefully placed the point on Thoma's throat, trying to stop his hand trembling. As an afterthought he said, 'Two of you others get hold of him and pull his head back tight.'

Two of them clasped the dying corporal's head in their hands and jerked it back to expose the skinny neck with its prominent adam's apple. Karl swallowed hard, desperately trying to remember what they had taught him about anatomy in the SPD Youth Movement.* He gritted his teeth, noting how Thoma's eyes were glazing over. He was dying visibly. Although his legs were trembling, Karl felt his hand steady. It was now or never. He thrust home the point of the bayonet and the blood welled out immediately. He knew he had to go deeper. But he had to watch out for the jugular vein. If he cut that . . . He dare not think that particular thought to its grim end.

Instead he widened the incision, praying that the other two would keep Thoma's head steady as he searched for the white cartliage of the trachea. Roused by the sudden new pain Thoma struggled like a fish trapped in a net. Desperately the two men clung to his head. Karl's eyes began to mist. The strain was too much. He felt he must faint at any moment. The weariness, the blood, the cold. Suddenly there it was, gleaming like ivory against the red gore. The trachea! He did not hesitate an instant. Placing the sharp point of the bayonet against the white tube, he pressed hard and slit downwards.

Thoma gave a great gasp. Air flooded his lungs. He gasped again. Almost magically the blackness began to vanish from his tortured face. The writhing and turning, desperate for air, vanished. With something akin to a weary smile on his face, Corporal Thoma slipped into unconsciousness, while Karl sat back on his heels absolutely, totally exhausted, the bayonet slipping from his nerveless fingers.

Ten minutes later they were being ushered into the first of the *Westwall* bunkers and the phone at Colonel von Heinersdorff's bedside was ringing yet again . . .

But exhausted as he was, Karl Carstens could not sleep that first day of Christmas, 1939, as the surgeons worked desperately to save Corporal Thoma's life. For an hour or two he tried to fight it, his mind racing electrically with the events of the night – the Frenchman he had killed, the singing Alsatians they had slaughtered, that desperate attempt to

*Pre-Hitler socialist youth organization.

save Corporal Thoma's life. But in the end he knew he wouldn't sleep this night. So as silently as he could, he slipped out of his bunk and left the blacked-out barracks room, loud with Polack's energetic snoring, to put his boots on outside in the corridor.

The *Adolf Hitler Kaserne* was silent, wreathed in the pre-dawn Christmas holiday torpor. There was no sound even from King Bull's kitchens. The sentries posted at the gate seemed to be part of the stonework, immobile, non-human, the only sign that they were really alive the grey fog of breath that came from them. It was as if he were the last man left alive in the whole wide world.

Shivering a little in the freezing air and tugging up his collar, a pensive Karl strolled aimlessly across the barracks square, reflecting on the terrible events of the night; where his father, whom he had not seen since the Gestapo had come for him in '38, might be at this moment; how his mother, the wife of a 'notorious folk-parasite', as the local *Kreisleiter** had denounced her publicly, would be managing on the little money she earned going out cleaning in Hamburg's wealthier suburbs . . .

Somehow Karl realized he had grown much older this night. It was not something that he could formulate easily, in spite of the quickness of his tongue. But life, suddenly, had grown even more complicated, yet at the same time very simple. A man's life could end so very suddenly; a random piece of lead and all the years he had put into life could be snuffed out in an instant. The thought made him soft and slack somehow, as if it didn't matter, as if nothing mattered very much.

Abruptly he remembered Corporal Thoma's words to him on that first day they had gone out to the observation post overlooking the Rhine together: *'Take the advice of an old hare, Carstens. If yer keep yer ass open and yer trap shut, yer turnip down and yer chin up, you might be lucky and end this frigging war as a civvie.'* His jaw tightened and he told himself the old noncom had

*Local Nazi official.

been right. You didn't have to submit, let yourself be used as cannonfodder, to die purposelessly like his comrades of the patrol had died this night. He wanted to end the war 'as a civvie' – and not a dead military hero. He glared at the grey gloom fiercely, as if challenging someone to deny that he was right.

It was just about then that he heard the aimless, almost casual footsteps behind him. Karl turned swiftly, wondering who would be out taking a stroll at this time of a Christmas morning. Someone was coming towards him slowly, coat draped across his shoulders casually, and Karl caught the whiff of cigar smoke. Then he recognized the figure and clicked to attention.

'Pill', for it was the regimental surgeon, an elderly kindly man, whose nickname had been gained from his fondness for handing out laxative pills for most internal disorders, raised his hand to his cap wearily and said, 'Happy Christmas, Grenadier.'

'Thank you, sir, the same to you,' Karl answered stiffly.

Pill stopped and peered a little short-sightedly at Karl in the gloom. 'Ah-ah,' he exclaimed, taking his cigar out of his mouth, 'you are one of the grenadiers who brought in old Corporal Thoma, aren't you, the one who did the job on his throat. Quick thinking that, my boy, by the way.'

'Yessir. Thank you, sir . . . May I be so bold as to ask how Corporal Thoma is doing, sir?'

Pill frowned. 'Hm,' he said, 'In spite of your sterling work, his injuries were too great. He died half an hour ago . . .'

And with that he was gone, leaving Karl feeling suddenly very old.

CHAPTER 8

ON THE day that the 'Führer's Holiday', as it had come to be called, ended, the survivors of the patrol across the Rhine were summoned to Creeping Jesus's office, including Ami, his arm in a sling, and now sporting the black wound medal.

It was another freezingly cold day, the sky leaden with the promise of more snow, and an icy wind was blowing in from the east. Hung over as most of the grenadiers still were from the three-day holiday with extra schnaps and beer, they hurried to and fro across the parade ground all the same; it was simply too cold to linger about. Even King Bull had vanished from his usual post, filling the doorway of the regimental kitchen, eyeing the happenings of the barracks square critically. Probably he was toasting his big feet at the nearest range, Karl told himself bitterly, as the adjutant continued to keep them waiting in the icy wind.

'What d'yer think the shitehawk wants us for?' Ami asked, his thin face blue with cold, his teeth chattering.

'Your medal . . . he wants to congratulate yer on your frigging medal!' Polack growled, his face set in a frown, as if the world in which he found himself puzzled him; which, in truth, it did most of the time.

'Screw your mother,' Ami said without rancour.

'Your grandmother, too,' Polack growled back, equally without rancour. The two of them often traded insults thus and there was never any bad blood between them: the lapsed, womanizing Catholic from the Rhineland and the big ex-farmer from Poland, with his Slavic intensity. The knowledge that they were secret rebels against a regime they hated kept them firm friends.

'Perhaps he's going to discharge you, Ami,' Karl ventured, smiling, 'on account of your wound. Think of it. Discharged! You'll sit around the local inn, full of piss and vinegar, showing off yer medal, telling the admiring citizens about your experiences in the big war. Think of all the gash –'

'All right, you lot!' a harsh voice cut into Karl's fantasies, 'the adjutant'll see yer now. Atten-*shun*!'

As one they snapped to attention and then they were marching into a well-heated office, the warmth striking their frozen faces like a flabby wet fist, to face Creeping Jesus who sat behind the desk with his cap on. He even wore grey dress gloves, a sign that this was a very formal occasion.

For what seemed a long time he kept them standing to attention in silence, as if he had forgotten they were there. In the outer office a typewriter clattered and a high-pitched affected voice was saying, 'Of course, it's far too good for the men. In my opinion, they're spoiling the other ranks. Making them soft . . .'

'A shockingly bad performance!' Creeping Jesus came to life suddenly. 'A disgrace to the Fourth Grenadiers. God only knows what division thinks of us now after that fiasco!' He growled with irritation and frowned at the rigid young men, while unconsciously his gloved fingers sought and touched his brand new Iron Cross, First Class, as if he wished to reassure himself that he had actually won the award.

They stared back at his silly affected face in bewilderment until they realized he was talking about the disastrous patrol across the Rhine which had cost the lives of nearly a score of their comrades. Karl flushed a little angrily. Was it their fault the operation had been a balls-up from the start?

Creeping Jesus rapped the paper in front of him with his knuckles. 'Preliminary report,' he barked. 'It shows that, with the exception of my own group which fought to the bitter end, your leaders panicked and that you retreated in complete disorder. The lot of you are damned lucky that division has not decided to press charges against you for cowardice in the face of the enemy!' Creeping Jesus's sallow features flushed with artificial rage.

Karl clenched his fists till it hurt. He thought of the young lieutenant shot at the door of the barn, Thoma with his chest ripped apart, and all the rest of those young men who had been killed purposelessly that Christmas Eve night; while somehow or other the pompous fool in front of him had managed to save his precious hide. Why was it that he, an officer, was the only man who had managed to rescue himself of the group left behind? Karl thought he knew how. Creeping Jesus had abandoned them to their fate in the confused fighting, had sneaked away like the coward he was and had somehow reached the German side of the Rhine. Now he was maligning good men who were dead and could not defend themselves. *It was damned unfair!*

'Your conduct is a blot on the Regiment. The Colonel has categorically refused to see you. You have shamed him and the Regiment with your lack of guts and fighting spirit. *In essence, you don't deserve to be grenadiers!*' He spat at them with such force that his monocle nearly popped out of his eye. 'If I had *my* way you'd be sent packing this very minute, off to a penal regiment, where in due course you would have your heads blown off, lifting mines or something stupid like that. It would be a fitting end - and a service to the country - for the lot of you.' He paused, skinny chest heaving with the effort of so much talk.

Karl felt his rage growing by the instant. Next to him Polack had begun to breathe harder, signalling his mounting anger, too. Even Ami, the most cynical of the three Rebels, grunted and cleared his throat noisily.

Creeping Jesus did not appear to notice the young men's anger. He snapped, 'As you are unworthy of the honour of being fighting soldiers, I am sending the lot of you back to the kitchens, where undoubtedly *Oberfeldwebel* Bulle will ensure, at least, that you work - and work hard - until the Colonel decides you have earned the privilege of returning to the ranks of the grenadiers. Now get out of my sight! I can't stand your stupid, cowardly faces any longer . . .'

'Welcome back to my kitchens,' King Bull said softly, a smile on his brick-red face which boded no good for the half-dozen shivering young men standing rigidly to attention in front of him in the glistening, immaculate kitchen. 'I suppose you think, after you ran away from the decadent frogs, you're gonna find a soft number back here in kind old King Bull's kitchen, eh?' His voice was full of menace now. 'Sugar titty and frigging finger-bowls, eh? Pea soup and pork sausage for breakfast, what? Coffee and cream frigging cakes every afternoon? Is that what yer thinking? Come on, out with it!'

Nervously they chorused as one, 'No sergeant.'

'*King Bull*!' he bellowed in his old furious manner, 'Won't you ever frigging well get it, *King Bull to you scum*! By the Great Whore of Buxtehude where the hounds bark with their tails, I'm gonna zap your lame asses from morning till frigging night. Why you mule-headed, rattle-brained, scrambled-eyed excuses for soldiers, I'm gonna show you what real terror is. Great buckets of flying crap, you're gonna go down on your bended knees and pray to me to let you go and have yer frigging stupid heads shot off by the frogs when I'm through with you . . .' They quailed visibly under that terrifying barrage of words, as King Bull pumped his huge chest ever larger so that it appeared it would inevitably explode. But it didn't and finally the big head cook ran out of breath. Gasping with the effort of so much shouting, he said huskily. 'Now go from my gaze, and if I have as much as to touch King Bull's whistle, heads will roll and the gutters'll drip with blood – *your* blood . . . NOW – GET OUT OF MY FRIGGING SIGHT!'

They fled.

Now as 1939 gave way to 1940 and the Western Front remained strangely quiet, the wretched survivors of that disastrous patrol led a miserable existence in King Bull's kitchens. For the latter knew of Creeping Jesus's hatred for these young men and did with them just as he pleased, safe in the knowledge that no one would listen to their complaints. Now he worked them to the absolute limit, constantly threatening them, urging them to ever greater efforts, piling on the work and pressure until they could hardly see straight for fatigue and staggered through their duties in those steaming noisy, echoing kitchens, as if they were drunk. Even when they had a few minutes off, he was always there, ranting to his cronies in that grating, booming voice of his, boasting as always of his sexual prowess, while they squatted morosely in a corner of the kitchen, sipping cold ersatz coffee and waiting for the murderous routine to commence once more.

'An ass is an ass,' he might pontificate, waving his mug of real coffee, laced with brandy, in front of his admiring crowd of senior cooks. 'But that ain't necessarily so. Take yer short-legged wench for example. Her ass I'd classify as a sand-digger.'

'Sand-digger?' one of them would ask, pretending surprise although they had heard all his stories many times before.

'*Jawohl*, sand-digger because it hangs so low that it digs a couple of grooves in the earth when its owner moves!'

And the little circle would erupt into fawning laughter.

'Why, by the time I was your lot's age, I'd won fourteen loving cups and eight medals for screwing. Women chased me from far and wide. Blondes, brunettes, red-heads. Some of them even paid me. It got so bad that I had one of my corporals keep the books for me, kind of like a secretary. After a month the little men in the rubber van had to come and take him away. It was too much for him - he had a nervous breakdown . . !' And off they would go, roaring with laughter again.

Drunk by now, as usual, he would clutch the front of his bulging trousers and declare, 'Gonna grab myself a piss now outside. Any one of you dangling ding-dongs who want to see what a real dong looks like - follow me out!' And he would stagger off, followed by the rest of the laughing cooks to spray the walls of the urinals, while the wretched fatigue men watched, hollow-eyed and resentful.

But it was not only his treatment of them which made the three Rebels resent and hate the head cook; it was also the knowledge that he was the lowest of the low: a thief who stole the rations of his comrades.

It was Karl who first spotted it. No matter how drunk or careless he was, King Bull never let the big key to the central storeroom out of his possession. Like the gleaming whistle it was on his person all the time he was in the kitchen. When it came time to issue the staples of the day to the cooks – the meats, sausages, coffee etc – it was King Bull personally who opened the door to the storeroom, weighed out the quantities and then, unlocking the door, handed them to the waiting cooks.

One day Karl was sent to collect the sausage for the green pea soup being served that midday. King Bull handed him the big bath filled to the top with the coils of red sausage, snapping: 'Now get that lot to the cooks at the double, Grenadier, and make my portion extra strong. I'm extra partial to green soup.' He raised his right flank and cracked off a great fart, grinning maliciously as he noted how Karl's face turned an ashen-white as the noxious smell wafted his way. 'Now at the double man!'

Bent double under that tremendous weight, Karl staggered off. But instead of going straight to the cooks, he lugged the bath to the scales in the next room, which was empty. Swiftly he weighed the coils, one by one, taking note of the exact weight. 'And do you know what I found out?' he told the other two Rebels grimly. 'The big bastard has given the cooks short weight. No wonder he does the weighing out and issuing himself, the big streak of piss. Three thousand men on strength, with fifty grams per man, so the weight should have been one hundred and fifty kilos. It wasn't. It was exactly one hundred and thirty kilos. So –'

'So he's organized,' Ami made a sweeping gesture with his hand, as if he were concealing something behind his back, 'twenty frigging kilos of prime pork sausage for hissen.'

'And I know where it's going to,' Polack growled. 'You know that fat taxi driver who brings up King Bull's current blonde every night of the week?'

They nodded.

'Well, just before he leaves, King Bull always hands him a big parcel of something on the sly. I bet you the taxi-driver is his go-between for the black market.' He clenched his big fist, dark eyes glowing fiercely, 'Oh, how I'd dearly love to give the bastard a real knuckle sandwich!' He licked his lips as if in anticipation of a good meal. 'The three of us could manage after dark when he's on his own. He's allus half-pissed by then.'

Karl shook his head, while Ami looked worried. 'No, that's not the way to do it, Polack. They'd find us out in the end and it'd be Torgau for us - striking a senior noncom, even a prick like King Bull, is a very serious offence. No, we've got to catch him with his hand in the till somehow.' He frowned. 'Show him up publicly.'

'The black market connection?' Ami suggested.

'Something like that -'

'What you three doing hiding behind them crates?' King Bull's tremendous bellow broke startlingly into their discussion, followed an instant later by another of his tremendous pea-soup farts. 'Bunch of nancy-boys, probably playing with yersens agen. Come on, hindlegs in yer flippers, there's a lot o' work to be done. *Move it!*' And he farted again.

'Tonight,' Karl hissed as they fled into the outer kitchen. *'We'll take the big bastard's drawers down for good tonight!'*

CHAPTER 9

BUT THAT wasn't to be – not yet.

On that very same afternoon that a farting King Bull accused the Three Rebels of being 'nancy-boys' who played with themselves, a *Luftwaffe* courier plane lost its way in thick cloud between the garrisons of Muenster and Cologne. With his petrol running desperately low, the worried pilot made a forced landing in a field. To his great surprise and the absolute consternation of his sole passenger, Major Helmut Reinberger of the *Luftwaffe* General Staff, they were not in the Reich; they had landed by mistake in neutral Belgium! Now khaki-clad figures, carrying long old-fashioned bayonets, were advancing upon them cautiously.

Reinberger, knowing that his career was probably already in ruins, perhaps even his very life forfeit, reacted desperately. 'Try to stop them!' he yelled to the bemused pilot and ran heavily through the damp grass to a clump of bushes. With fingers that trembled violently, he poured the contents of his bulging briefcase, which had been handcuffed to his wrist, on to the ground, fumbled with his lighter, clicking the wheel angrily, trying to strike a light.

'La! Dans les arbres!' The Belgian soldiers spotted the first thin flames as the papers began to ignite.

The pilot held out his arms in an attempt to stop him. Excitedly the Belgians brushed him to one side and doubled towards the little fire. A minute later they were stamping out the flames with their heavy boots while Major Reinberger watched them, near to tears . . .

An ashen-faced, unshaven Reinberger swallowed hard and then answered the general's question. 'I succeeded in burning them, sir, to insignificant fragments,' he made a weak gesture, 'the size of the palm of my hand.'

General Jodl's pale, clever face creased into a frown. For

what appeared to be a long time, he remained silent as he considered the crestfallen officer's statement. Reinberger waited impatiently. His chief, Air Marshal Goering, sitting behind his desk in his dove-grey uniform like a tethered barrage balloon, had already warned him he might well have to 'take the officer's way out'; he meant shoot himself for his failure to prevent the vital documents falling into foreign hands.

Finally Hitler's Chief-of-Staff broke the heavy brooding silence. 'I am afraid Major Reinberger that we cannot discount the fact that the Belgians may now be in possession of some of our plan of attack. Half an hour ago, we heard that they have put into operation, what they call Phase Two, the next-to-last step in the mobilization of their Army. They have also called up two new classes of reservists.' He shrugged. 'I think I need say no more. Thank you, however, for coming.' With that he bent his head over his documents, the Major already forgotten. Reinberger snapped to attention, saluted and went out. He had been condemned to death.

For a long time the General pondered what he should advise the Führer, as the shadows lengthened outside the Reich Chancellery, and five hundred kilometres south of Berlin, three humble grenadiers prepared for their confrontation with a certain crooked noncom. The Führer had decided the great attack on the west would be launched against France through neutral Belgium and Luxembourg this very month. Now he was quite sure, Brussels, neutral that it was, would inform Paris and London of the German intentions. Even if they had managed to seize only part of the plans which that fool Reinberger had failed to destroy, it would suffice. As a result the French and English would pack France's border with Belgium with troops and the right-wing hook, which the Greater General Staff had planned to sweep round behind the Maginot Line would meet with resistance almost as soon as it started. No, the attack west was out of the question this month!

Jodl pursed his thin lips. Outside there was no sound save the steady tramp of the black-clad sentries on the concrete. In spite of the emergency, most of the staff had gone home at the usual time.

But one day, this month, the next month, the one afterwards, the plan of attack on France would have to be put into operation. It was the only one that did not entail a head-on attack on the damned Maginot Line. How could he convince the Western Allies then, that the Reinberger plan was *not* the one which would be used by the *Wehrmacht* one day? Perhaps if the German Army commenced operations in another area altogether, the enemy might believe that the documents the Belgians had presumably shown them were a 'plant'. In the Old War, both sides had carefully ensured that 'key plans' had been found on the bodies of dead officers discovered on the battlefield in order to confuse the other side as to its real intentions. Jodl frowned. Outside they were beginning to draw the heavy velvet blackout curtains. The Führer would be indulging himself in his usual peppermint tea and heavy, cream-laden Viennese cakes soon, with the usual predictable results. His totally ruined stomach would act up on him and his advisers would have to sit there, listening to him break wind the whole time, pretending they had not noticed a thing, though the stench that came from the most powerful man in Europe was nauseating. He, Jodl, must make up his mind what to say before that happened. His own stomach was also very sensitive.

Jodl thought of the other operation which the Greater General Staff was currently planning. It was not as important as the great attack on the west; yet all the same, its success would guarantee the Reich's vital ore base in Sweden, without which Germany's war industry would soon grind to a halt for the lack of iron ore. Its success would also give the Navy and Air Force a wider starting line for their operations against the damned English.

In a way the operation was designed to appear as a *peaceful* occupation the object of which was to protect the neutrality of the states Germany would invade. But Jodl suspected the

Wehrmacht would meet resistance, at least in one of the states, and *there would be fighting*!

Through the great oaken door, Jodl heard the soft, muted boom of the gong which indicated that '*Kaffeetrinken*', as it was traditionally called although the Führer only drank herbal tea, was soon to be served. It was time to see the Führer before those rich cakes were devoured and, the laxatives which invariably followed them had their usual unpleasant effect upon Hitler's digestive system.

Hurriedly he did up the buttons of his tunic and collected his papers, his mind made up. He would recommend two actions to the Führer. An instant alert on the Western Front, freezing all German troops the length of the Reich's border with France and Belgium in their battle positions for the next twenty-four hours; and an immediate change in operations to the attack in the north. With luck he'd fool the enemy on both fronts, and the great attack on the west would come, in due course, as a surprise after all. Pleased with himself, he dismissed the flunkey guarding the great door and opened it himself to reveal Adolf Hitler greedily dipping his finger into the thick whipped cream on the nearest cake, and announced at the top of his voice: '*Mein Führer*, momentous news, all is not lost . . .'

The most powerful man in Europe looked up startled like a schoolboy caught dipping his hand in the sweets jar . . .

'*Now*!' Karl hissed, as the fat taxi-driver began to lug the heavy parcel King Bull had just given him across the snow, puffing and panting, his bulk outlined by the yellow shaft of light escaping from the blacked-out door.

Polack dashed forward, sawn-off table-leg raised. But in the very same instant that the big grenadier prepared to bring it down on the unsuspecting black marketeer's head, buglers shrilled the alarm. Abruptly whistles were blowing, NCOs ripping open doors and shouting orders, officers yelling '*stand to . . . stand to everyone*' and Karl knew with a sinking feeling that the balloon had gone up at last . . .

BOOK TWO

The Battle of the Kitchens

'Buy combs, lads . . . There are lousy times ahead!'

The Sayings of Karl Carstens

CHAPTER 1

'*Himmelherrgott!*' Colonel von Heinersdorff moaned in dismay. Hastily he reined back his horse, holding the bit tight in order to prevent the bay from shying at the burning village in front of him. Behind, the battalion which had been so hastily alerted stumbled to a stop, the men gasping with the effort of the forced march.

An old woman lay in the snow, dead, her skirts thrown up to reveal her naked yellow thighs. Besides her two children sprawled in grotesque poses, both their throats cut.

Next to Karl, a young soldier choked with horror and then turning to one side, vomited into the ditch, shoulders heaving violently.

'My God,' Polack breathed as the cracked old colonel continued to stare down at the old woman and the two children, as if he could not believe the evidence of his own eyes, 'they've raped the old woman!'

'But the French wouldn't rape old women!' Karl objected, as the battalion waited for the colonel to decide what should be done.

'Don't you believe it,' Ami said darkly. 'You don't know what they're like. When they occupied us till twenty-nine, you had to watch those black Senegalese of theirs. Big black bastards. Screw anything with hair on! And them Arabs of theirs were even worse. They liked little boys and –'

'Be quiet in the ranks back there!' Creeping Jesus ordered angrily, rising in his stirrups, trying to get a better view of the burning village in the first thin rays of the morning sun, praying that the French patrol which had crossed the Rhine last night had gone back the way it had come.

Colonel von Heinersdorff waved his broken sword. 'Third and Fourth Companies take left and right flank! First and Second Companies follow me,' he commanded, breath fogging on the cold air. 'At the double now!' He urged his horse into a trot.

As the two rear companies spread out to left and right in the snowy fields, the first two companies pushed forward at a run, boots clattering on the glistening cobbles. Karl, running heavily with the rest, shook his head in disbelief. 'Shit,' he gasped. 'If the frogs are still in that village, we're gonna walk right into it. That old horned-ox up front needs his head seeing to!'

It was the same thought that had just occurred to Creeping Jesus. 'Men lagging to the rear, sir,' he barked. 'See there are no stragglers, sir?'

'Good idea, von Schorr!'

Creeping Jesus waited for no further orders. He wheeled his horse round and cantered towards the end of the column, where he would be safe.

They doubled past the first of the blazing half-timbered houses. Two dead peasants stood propped up against a horse trough. In a kind of brutal, macabre joke, someone had cut the man's genitals off and thrust them into the dead woman's mouth, as if she were sucking an obscene lollipop. The men muttered angrily and Karl felt a burning rage sweep through him. For the very first time since he had joined the Fourth Grenadiers, he wanted to kill somebody - badly. They ran on.

There was a sudden rattle, louder than the crackle of the timbers burning on both sides of the street, like an idle urchin running an iron bar along some railings. The running men faltered to a clumsy stop instinctively. Angry blue sparks were running across the cobbles straight towards them. Colonel von Heinersdorff stared at the slugs as if he couldn't quite believe that someone was actually firing at *him*! Suddenly he raised himself in his stirrups, waved his broken sword and cried. 'Remember the honour of the regiment, Fourth Grenadiers . . . *ATTACK*!'

Crying hoarsely, the young grenadiers streamed forward awkwardly, packed together, but impelled by some wild animal fury that made them forget all fear. Drunk as they were on looted schnaps, the giant black Senegalese dug in the *Rathaus** could not miss. The First Company was ripped apart. In an instant great gaps appeared in their ranks. Men fell everywhere, yelling with rage, crying piteously for help. The Colonel's horse went down on its forelegs, blood arcing scarlet jets from its shattered side. Von Heinersdorff slammed to the cobbles, unconscious. A lieutenant ran past him towards the machine-gun spitting blue fire. His chest was torn apart. Still he staggered on, carried forward by the crazed illogical energy of men in combat. He fell to his knees, thrusting his shattered chest against its red-hot muzzle effectively blocking its fire for a few moments until a giant Senegalese, his glistening black face disfigured by ritual scars, slammed his brass-shod rifle butt against the back of his head. The body flew away.

But the officer's sacrifice had been in vain. Everywhere what was left of the First Company was frantically scrambling for cover, while behind them the Second Company, its progress blocked by the dead, milled around leaderlessly and totally confused. The unlucky Fourth Grenadiers were living up to their reputation . . .

Polack knocked off the head of the bottle, took a deep swig, spat out the broken glass and wordlessly handed it to Ami, who squatted next to him in the cellar. Beside him, Karl wiped the sweat from his forehead and peered out through the cobwebbed grating.

The street, which was at eye-level, was littered with dead and wounded grenadiers, twitching with acute agony as their bodies were struck again, as the Senegalese relentlessly hosed the street with machine-gun fire. Valiantly the dying horse tried to fight its way up onto its legs, while beside it its master lay motionless, dead or unconscious, Karl didn't know or care. His whole attention was concentrated on those black bastards firing the machine-gun from the *Rathaus*. Ami

*Town Hall.

handed him the bottle. He too took a swig, hardly noticing what he drank, mind still on that machine-gun. At that moment it seemed the most important thing in the world.

'What we gonna do, Karl?' Polack asked and then repeated his question when his handsome pale-faced comrade did not seem to hear.

'Get that frigging gun!' Karl replied, baring his teeth wolfishly. Ami stared at him in the dark cellar curiously, but said nothing. 'There must be some way of working our way round their frigging backs into the *Rathaus*.'

Polack nodded and reached for his bayonet.

Ami wet his lips nervously, feeling that he was being overtaken by events and not liking it one bit. 'But unless this is a full-scale invasion, they'll be pulling back across the Rhine soon and we'll . . .' His words trailed away helplessly. Karl was not listening.

'*We must attack, sir*!' the wounded lieutenant said desperately, near to tears, as the other walking wounded streamed by the two of them. 'What's left of the First Company is trapped in the village.' He shook his head and gobs of blood, thick and black, from the deep wound in his ashen cheek fell to the snow like red rain.

'It can only be a patrol,' a terrified Creeping Jesus reasoned, just as Ami had. 'They're using the new alert in the north to put pressure on us here. They'll pull back soon, believe you me.'

'But sir –'

'All right, young Krueger,' Pill's calm voice butted in. 'Let's be having you.' He made the boy roll up his right sleeve and pressed home the morphia injection with hands that were red with blood right up to the wrists. Hastily he pencilled the dosage given on the wounded officer's forehead and gently urged him to the waiting ambulance, packed with its cargo of moaning, badly wounded men.

Creeping Jesus gulped and did not dare look. They reminded him just how frail the human body was. Again he considered the problem, still angry at that damned fool of a colonel for going and getting himself killed. Both flank attacks had been stalled, as had the one the colonel had led himself. He knew that the right tactic now was to group the remaining two companies, wheel behind the blazing village and block the route the damned French would have to use for their withdrawal to the Rhine. But the grenadiers were badly rattled and would need firm leadership. That would mean he would have to command them – and he did not like that prospect one bit.

But if he did nothing and it came out, there would be trouble, an inquiry, even a court-martial. After the business of that disastrous patrol he had been able to fool von Heinersdorff, but his luck wouldn't hold out a second time. He had to do something! He bit his bottom lip and tried not to look at the straggler, reeling from side to side, his jaw shot away, the bits of broken bone gleaming like polished ivory in the scarlet mess. Suddenly he had it. As in the distance the sirens began to sound their shrill warning, the agreed signal for a French attack on the Red Zone*, he knew it would be only a matter of time before the French withdrew; the whole area being alerted. So, if he appeared to be doing something, they might well be gone before he actually had to attack. He crooked a finger at his sergeant and cried above the wail of the air-raid sirens, 'Sergeant Maltz . . . at the double!'

'Sir?'

'Back to the barracks, as soon as you can. Alert Second and Third Battalions, clerks, cooks, everyone who can fire a rifle.' Hastily he scribbled an order on his pad and thrust at the sergeant. 'Up here at once.' He flashed a glance at his watch. 'The Regiment counter-attacks at ten hundred hours precisely. Now remember, *everybody*, Sergeant.'

'Sir!' The sergeant turned and began to run back down the road, as if he were training for the Olympics.

Creeping Jesus smiled thinly to himself. He relaxed against the nearest tree and took a hand-rolled cigarette from his

*Code name given to the German border area.

silver case. He was out of danger. By the time they had gathered the rest of the regiment together, including the clerks and cooks who probably wouldn't even know where their weapons were, the French would have evacuated the village and be back across the Rhine. He savoured the smoke, obviously well pleased with himself, as the wounded streamed by. He had solved the problem. *He* would see no action this day . . . In the village the slaughter continued.

Karl crouched on the slippery roof, his rifle slung, the grenades he had taken off the dead stuck down the sides of his jackboots. Behind him Polack pushed Ami cautiously through the dirty fanlight.

Now the chatter of the machine-gun had almost ceased. For the last ten minutes the Senegalese had systematically slaughtered the wounded down below in the street. Only a few were left, twitching feebly as they bled to death. Karl controlled his rage at the senseless slaughter of defenceless men and began to edge his way along the roof, concealed from below by the central ridge. As was usual in these medieval villages of the Rhine, each house was interlocked, with only an occasional break between them. With a bit of luck, they'd be able to come down behind the *Rathaus* unseen, though Ami had been decidedly nervous. 'They're as steep as hell, them roofs. Yer could slip easily. It's easy for you to talk,' he had objected, 'you was a tiler, Karl.'

But now even he wasn't finding it too frightening, after Karl had explained that these old medieval houses all had fire-hooks fixed in their timbers so that you could use them as convenient hand-holes.

Now they progressed rapidly, stopped only by a gap between houses over which Polack and Karl together managed to haul a pale-faced Ami. Once Karl chanced a glance over the edge of the roof. Below a white officer, scarf wound around his neck, white *kepi* set at a jaunty angle, followed by half a dozen gigantic Senegalese in red fezzes, was going from body to body, checking if they were dead by kicking them in the ribs. Karl was tempted to throw his grenades there and then. He caught himself in time and crawled on.

They came to a bend in the line of red roofs. Karl took a look. He was right. The street they were working their way along was curving behind the *Rathaus*. They were no longer in the frogs' sights. With a bit of luck, it would be safe to go down now. 'I'm going to go down,' he hissed to the other two, as the firing ceased altogether now and at the far end of the village bugles commenced shrilling.

'Watch it, Karl,' Polack whispered in warning.

Karl forced a smile. 'Don't worry, Polack, I'm gonna knock out that shitting gun to make them pay for what they did to our poor fellows - then my days as a hero are over. Here I go . . .'

CHAPTER 2

'I'VE WRAPPED you a packet of cheese sandwiches and a canteen of nigger sweat, *Oberfeld*,' Corporal Tietze said fawning, as outside soldiers ran back and forth and NCOs bellowed urgent commands.

King Bull hurriedly changing into clean underwear, spun round on him, tin pan in hand, 'Have you got air in your tooth?' he demanded angrily. 'What have you got up there in yer turnip – frigging porridge?'

Tietze fell back a pace. 'But what have I done wrong, *Oberfeld*?' He whined like a housewife who can never do anything right for a man.

King Bull did not answer for a moment. Instead he concentrated on trying to fix the small pan into the flies of his long woollen underpants. Outside the hurriedly alerted officers were cantering up on their horses. All was haste and noise. The pan fixed securely over his most vital parts, King Bull slipped into his uniform and then, as an afterthought, he tucked his metal shaving mirror into his tunic pocket to cover his heart, while Tietze watched him a little bewildered. 'Do you know what happens to a soldier who gets a bullet in his belly when he's wearing dirty underwear and his guts are full of fodder, Tietze?' he asked, reaching for his helmet.

'No, *Oberfeld*.'

'I'll tell yer – for free. He gets gas gangrene, that's what he gets. Yer swell up! Yer flesh rots! Yer stink!'

Tietze swallowed hard and turned pale as King Bull warmed to the subject with morbid fascination, forgetting his own fears for a moment.

'The pong is horrible. They can smell yer stink for a couple of kilometres and the sawbones have got to keep cutting more and more of yer flesh away.' He paused and tapped the tin can inside his trousers reassuringly. 'And you frigging well want me to eat a cheese sandwich!' He shook his cropped head at the stupidity of his fellow human beings and strapped on his pistol. 'Come on, arse-with-ears, let's get them thieving hash-slingers moving.'

Outside they were unloading more wounded from the old boxlike ambulances. The walking wounded zig-zagged as if they were drunk towards the aid post, taking small mincing steps, faces grey with shock at this outrage done to their bodies, their eyes wide and unseeing. The more serious cases lay still in their stretchers, some moaning softly, others unconscious, the blood dripping from the canvas onto the snow. King Bull watched mutely, unaffected by the suffering of the men who were his comrades. Standing next to him, Corporal Tietze wondered if he was as afraid as he was. But he was wrong. King Bull was not afraid of being hurt, save perhaps for some injury to his sexual organs; for he had long regarded himself as 'the best swordsman in the frigging Fourth Grenadiers', if not in the whole division. Being wounded was for other, lesser mortals; it would interfere with his love life; his business interests; his command of those kitchens of which he was so proud. Suddenly the alarming thought flashed through the big man's mind that if he were wounded, he would lose command of his kingdom, the regimental kitchens of the Fourth Grenadiers. Someone else would undoubtedly take them over and his gravy-train days would be over. King Bull frowned hard, as the officers trotted to the heads of the waiting companies and the two battalions prepared to move off for the counter-attack. His frown changed to a look of anger and he doubled his big fists. No one, he promised himself as the battalion commander raised himself in his stirrups to cry, 'First Battalion – forward *march*!' was going to take his kitchens from him. Come what may in the next few hours, King Bull was not going to lose his kingdom. Then they were marching, eight hundred excited, frightened young men, towards the burning horizon . . .

Karl lowered himself down to the yard, littered with abandoned German equipment and the smashed household goods the Senegalese had looted and then thrown away. In his right hand he clenched the stick grenade, his heart beating hard, every nerve tingling, ready to act at the first sign of trouble.

Beyond the *Rathaus*, the white officer was attempting to form up the grinning drunken black giants, occasionally lashing out with the riding crop he affected when they appeared reluctant. But the gunners who had massacred the First Company were still in position. Obviously they were going to cover the withdrawal to the river until the last moment.

'In a pig's eye!' Karl told himself angrily. He'd make them pay for the massacre if it was the last thing he ever did.

Polack and Ami edged up to him, as he eyed the stretch of open ground between him and the rear entrance to the *Rathaus*. 'Do you think somebody's covering it?' Polack hissed, putting Karl's thoughts of that moment into words.

'Let's find out,' Karl answered. He took off his helmet and raised it cautiously over the low wall with his stick grenade. He had once seen someone do that in a pre-war film. Nothing happened. 'All right,' he gasped, realizing that he was panting suddenly, 'here I go!'

Polack crossed himself and said a swift prayer for his safety in Polish.

Abruptly Karl was on his feet and pelting across the littered yard, arms pumping like pistons, going all out. A moment later Polack followed. Then Ami. Nobody spotted them.

Stick grenades clutched in hands that were wet with sweat, the three of them cautiously opened the back door to the *Rathaus*. Their nostrils were assailed by the stale smell of the place, mixed with the strong odour of garlic and the coarse tobacco the French smoked.

The place was a shambles. The Senegalese had gone wild, smashing everything in an orgy of crazy destruction. Viewing all, Hitler, with his eyes gouged out by a bayonet, hung crazily from the bullet-pocked wall.

Gingerly, very gingerly, they crossed the room, wincing every time their feet crunched over the broken glass. Once they circled a fat man, whose belly had been ripped open savagely, his dead face muffled in a torn swastika flag. Now they could hear the drunken chatter of the gunners behind the door to their immediate front. They stole forward on tiptoe and paused. Ami thrust his grenade in his boot and poised with his hands on the handle. Karl nodded his approval, and pulled the china pin from the grenade. Polack did the same. Very deliberately, mouthing the numbers silently, Karl began to count. On three, Ami flung open the door. The other two didn't hesitate. They tossed in their grenades as Ami rammed the door closed again, ears deaf to the furious cries of alarm and surprise from within. For one long moment nothing happened. Abruptly there was a muffled crack, followed by a tremendous roar. The door bucked and jerked as Ami held on desperately. Smoke poured from beneath it. Karl gasped for breath. '*Now*!' he cried. Ami flung it open again. They rushed into the smoke-filled room. A Senegalese, shattered arm pumping dark-red blood, stumbled towards them, coughing thickly. Polack lashed out with his cruelly-shod boot. The Senegalese slammed into the wall, hanging there helplessly, as if glued to it, before beginning to slither its length, smearing the plaster crimson.

Another was attempting to escape up the rickety stairs. Karl fired from the hip. He jack-knifed. Next moment he was reeling backwards, hands flailing the air for a hold.

Karl blundered through the smoke-filled, shattered room, ears already taking in the cries of alarm and surprise from outside in the street. He pushed the writhing gunner to one side. His mate was already slumped dead and armless over the gleaming belt of cartridges.

Outside the officer in the white *kepi* was yelling orders and pointing to the *Rathaus* with his riding crop. Already some of the black giants were lurching forward, bayonets levelled, bodies bent like men beating their way through heavy rain.

Karl's fingers sought desperately for the firing button. He prayed that there would be no stoppage; they wouldn't stand a chance if there were. He pressed the button. The Hotchkiss sprang into violent life under his fingers. The muzzle spat bullets in a deadly arc. Karl spun it from left to right, the slugs being eaten up at a tremendous rate. Next to him Polack shoved the dead loader aside and seized another belt.

To their front the Senegalese were galvanized into crazy action. Their arms and legs flailing wildly they went down in a twitching, writhing heap like puppets in the hands of a master who had suddenly gone mad. Behind them their comrades fell back fearfully, jabbering excitedly among themselves, pointing at the window from which the firing was coming.

Crying furiously, their white officer tried to rally them, slashing at their backs with his riding crop, exposing himself recklessly.

Karl didn't waste the opportunity. He spun the gun round, steam wreathing its glowing muzzle. Next to him Polack fed in another belt. Karl squinted along the sight. It neatly dissected the angry young officer berating his sullen giants. For a moment he hesitated. The Frenchman was so young, so brave, so obviously eager for glory. Then he remembered all those other young men who had been slaughtered so cruelly in the main street and his jaw hardened. Breathing out very softly, he pressed the trigger and kept his finger there - hard.

The cry the Frenchman gave out was almost inhuman, as the cruel burst ripped his back to shreds. For a moment he simply hung there, the blood streaming down his shattered back, one shoulder hunched, standing on his toes like someone preparing to do the high jump. Suddenly - startlingly - his white *kepi* tumbled to the ground and his body slumped, as if suddenly drained of all energy - as if a tap had been opened abruptly. Without another sound he went down in a heap and made no further movement.

The officer's death seemed to act as a signal for the Senegalese. They drew back a few paces, some of them licking their thick lips with purple tongues, milling around, undecided what to do next.

Karl fired again. It did the trick. Someone shouted in thick unrecognizable French '*Shof ki po.*'* They panicked. Now they shoved, jostled and ripped at one another in their fear, trying to get away from that terrible machine-gun. Some even threw away their long rifles in their panic. They backed off, mumbling '*Shof ki po . . . Shof ki po,*' as if it were some tribal chant. '*Run for your lives! SHOF KI PO . . .*'

Karl sat back on his heels and watched them flee, suddenly sick of the killing, all emotion spent, as beside him Polack whispered, 'Poor black bastards . . . I wonder if they even know where they are, France . . . Germany? A strange cold place with a lot of white faces?'

'You'll make me frigging blub in half a mo,' Ami sneered. 'The black buggers might not know where they're frigging at, but they know how to loot, rape and kill all right. Believe you me.' He took up one of the wine bottles abandoned by the Senegalese attackers and took a tentative swig. 'Well, they didn't piss in the bottle at least,' he said grudgingly.

Wearily Karl rose to his feet and wiped the cold sweat from his forehead. 'Come on, you two. They've gone. Let's see if we can help any of those poor sods outside. There might be some of them still alive . . .'

Wordlessly they trooped out into the cold street, littered with the still bodies in field-grey. It had begun to snow again. Sad soft flakes were drifting down, as if some god on high had decreed that man's inhumanity to man should be hidden away as quickly as possible. Miserably they started to check the shattered bodies, shoulders bent as if in defeat . . .

* *'Sauve qui peut.'*

CHAPTER 3

CAPTAIN VON Schorr was delighted. The French were running, the reconnaissance report had stated. For some reason they had abandoned the village they had captured so surprisingly and were scattering everywhere, almost as if in panic. The cycle recce patrol was certain that there was no coherent command among the fleeing French. Many of them did not even seem to be heading for the Rhine. A few had actually been spotted heading straight for the main line of the *Westwall*, heading for certain death!

'Well, gentlemen,' he rasped to the two disappointed battalion commanders, 'it looks as if we've got a mopping up operation on our hands and not a concerted counter-attack. I suggest, *meine Herren*, that you march your chaps straight down to the Rhine, seal off, say, three kilometres to the right and left of the Gambsheim bridge and just wait for them to walk into your arms!' He beamed at them happily.

The two commanders were not quite convinced. Schmitz, the bigger of the two, frowned and said, 'Eight hundred men strung over three kilometres of ground . . . bit thin, you know, von Schorr, what!'

The other nodded his head in agreement.

Von Schorr rode over their objections easily, relaxed and confident now. 'Well, I'll leave it to you gentlemen and your tactical discretion. I think it's my duty to take up the rest of the First to the village,' he indicated the smoking ruins on the horizon, now strangely silent, 'and see what has happened to the rest of the men.' He looked pensive, as if he were moved. 'Must find the Colonel's body, you know. The honour of the Fourth Grenadiers and all that, gentlemen.'

Hastily the other two agreed, returned von Schorr's hasty salute, and then cantered off to their respective battalions to issue their orders.

Thus it was that an hour later King Bull and his handful of

freezing cooks, unhappy and not a little scared, found themselves digging into the bank of the Rhine. Even King Bull was subdued, as he dug effortlessly with the rest, puffing his black cigar. Visibility was decreasing by the instant, as the snowstorm grew in strength. Now it lashed the cooks' faces, making them gasp and splutter as they swallowed the icy flakes, covering their bent shoulders in a white mantle.

Finishing his own hole, King Bull barked, 'Move it, you lot. We don't want them black niggers to catch us with our drawers down when they come, do we!'

He flung down his shovel and flicked open the flap of his pistol holster, as Tietze quavered, 'Do you really think they'll come this way, *Oberfeld*?'

'Of course, they won't plush-ears! They wouldn't dare, with King Bull guarding this sector.' He swelled out his mighty chest, listening to the clang of the tin pot against his metal fly buttons. 'I'm going up top to have a look-see and I want them holes finished by the time I come back – *or else*!'

King Bull clambered up the frozen embankment, ducking his head deeper into his collar, as the snowflakes beat furiously against his face. The storm was becoming even worse. They were in for another heavy fall, he told himself a little gloomily. The damned winter seemed as if it would never come to an end!

He stamped about, head tucked deep into his collar, gloved hand clamped on his pistol, surrounded by a white wall of raging snowflakes. He wiped the snow from his eyes and decided it was time he got back to the holes. At least there would be a little shelter from the elements there. Suddenly to his horror, he realized he did not know in which direction the embankment lay. The whirling snow had obliterated his tracks. Were his men over there? Or perhaps over there?

King Bull stumbled to a stop, broad face very worried, hand instinctively gripping the butt of his pistol. '*Shit, shit, shit*!' he cursed to himself. Where were those shitting hash-slingers of his? It was as if he were the only man left in the world. He cupped his hand to his mouth and called softly, 'Hello, where are you?' There was no answer save for the shriek of the snow-laden wind. He called again, hardly daring to raise his voice any higher, as if he feared the French were lurking everywhere. 'Where are you, you plush-earred bastards?'

Still no reply. He staggered on a few paces until he blundered into a clump of firs. Their branches lashed his anxious face cruelly. He yelped with pain and stopped again. He was going around in circles. He had just passed the firs moments before. He could barely make out his own footprints, swiftly being obliterated by the snow which was coming down now in a solid white wall. He gulped hard and tried to think.

He could not be more than metres away from the Rhine. He had only walked for five minutes or so while they had finished the foxholes – and at a leisurely pace. Now the great river should be to the south, so where was north? Frantically he tried to remember what he had been taught in map-reading as a recruit; how to find north at night when there was no sun to guide you. His eyes lit up. Now he knew. Swiftly he bent down, half-blinded by the whirling snow, and felt the trunk of the nearest fir. There it was! The moss which grew on the northern side of the tree. If he walked in the opposite direction to the moss, he'd find the river and his men. His fear fled from him and he straightened his shoulders resolutely. By the Great God and All His Triangles, he promised himself grimly, wouldn't he turn them all into scarlet sows for having failed to answer him just now!

Carefully he set off again, bracing his big body against the howling wind, taking it step by step, body warmed by the knowledge of what he was going to do to his hash-slingers once he found them again. He'd zap their good-for-nothing asses for them, good and proper. His dripping, brick-red face cracked into a cold smile at the thought of the revenge he would exact; he'd work their asses off until –

He stopped abruptly, the smile vanishing as soon as it had come, cocking his head to one side in order to hear better. A strange sort of hoarse cry was coming from his right, almost like some sort of chant; like the frigging monks sang when they weren't playing with the five-fingered widow, which was most of the time. It sounded like '*Sho ki po*'.

Yes, definitely, that was it! *Sho ki po . . . AND IT WAS GETTING CLOSER . . .*

King Bull trembled.

'The colonel, sir,' reported the fat corporal, now minus his glasses, a livid weal ripped down the side of his pale face, indicating that the three Rebels should put down the stretcher, on which the snow-shrouded CO lay, still clasping his broken sword, not a mark on him, almost as if he had just fallen into a gentle sleep.

Gratefully the three comrades, who had found the colonel still alive among the dead of the village street, placed him down and groaned with relief.

Creeping Jesus said, 'Thank God he is safe,' aloud. Inside he cursed that the old fool hadn't snuffed it after all. Von Heinersdorff, unfortunately, was still going to remain a mortal danger to the men of the Fourth Grenadiers in general, and to himself in particular. 'Now we must get him to the aid station immediately.'

'The ambulance is already full, sir,' the fat corporal objected, his face lashed by the snow-heavy wind that howled down the village street, fanning the embers into flame once again. He indicated the vehicle packed with blood-stained, groaning men, the last survivors of the First Company.

Creeping Jesus did not seem to hear. 'It is imperative that the CO receives skilled medical attention at once,' he rasped, staring down at the colonel's silly face with feigned concern. 'Put him inside and order the driver to leave at once, Corporal.'

The fat corporal gulped, while the three Rebels stared dully at the noncom and the officer, wondering that they would do.

'There's some pretty badly wounded men in there, sir,' the corporal said a little lamely. 'They ought to be seen to at once, sir and the CO doesn't look too bad, like.'

Creeping Jesus looked at him coldly. 'Since when have you been a doctor, Corporal?' he barked. 'Get on with it and don't argue.'

Shoulders bent, the fat corporal turned to the three Rebels. 'Well, you heard the officer,' he said without enthusiasm. 'What yer waiting for – a written invite? Start unloading the amubulance.'

Nothing happened. Wordlessly the three of them stood their ground, as if by some trick of mental telepathy they had agreed not to carry out the adjutant's order.

The fat corporal looked at their wind-lashed faces helplessly, while von Schorr waited, slapping his cane against the side of his highly polished riding boot. 'Have you lot been eating big beans or someat?' he tried. 'Have yer got soil in yer spoons? *Didn't you hear me?*'

'We heard you all right, Corporal,' Karl said calmly.

'Then why didn't you carry out my order?' the NCO cried in exasperation.

'Because we don't think it's right or fair,' Karl answered, voice level and normal. 'The others are wounded as well. They need a good chance, just like the CO.'

Creeping Jesus shoved the fat corporal aside roughly. 'Carstens, isn't that your damned name, Grenadier Carstens?' he demanded angrily.

Karl clicked to attention. 'Yessir, that's my name,' he answered a little weakly, knowing what was to come.

Creeping Jesus thrust this face close to Karl's so that the latter could smell the expensive cologne which he used. 'Now listen to me, *Grenadier Carstens*,' he hissed threateningly. 'When I give an order, I expect it to be obeyed, and obeyed without question! Is that quite clear?'

Karl stood his ground, the wind whipping his battered uniform against his skinny frame, his face taut but resolute as the snowstorm shrieked about the two of them, isolating them from the rest. 'When somebody is wounded, sir, I think rank is no longer important. What is important is how badly wounded the man is, not whether he is an officer or another rank.'

Creeping Jesus opened his mouth to make an angry retort and then closed it again, as if somehow he had sensed just how resolute this young man facing him was. Threats would be of no avail. Instead he turned to the fat corporal and said, 'Get the CO off the stretcher, corporal, and into the cab of the ambulance. There's room for him there. See the driver starts at once for the barracks.'

'Yessir,' the fat corporal answered, happy that the matter had passed over without any trouble.

For a while Creeping Jesus seemed to forget the three Rebels, watching as the fat corporal heaved the CO's dead weight into the cab and then tumbled inside himself. A moment later the driver started up and the heavily laden ambulance started to slither and skid along in the new snow. Now the adjutant turned to face a waiting Karl. 'I am taking into consideration, Grenadier Carstens, that you and your comrades found and brought in the CO, possibly at some risk to yourself, I don't know, nor do I care.' He slapped his cane against his boot. 'Possibly the strain of combat here has had some effect on your attitude to authority, and I am prepared to forgive it this once. But never let it happen again.'

Karl stared back at the weak-chinned officer apparently calmly, though his mind was racing. First he had been forced into killing another fellow human being on that patrol with Corporal Thoma, he told himself. Then he had voluntarily striven to kill the black men who had slaughtered the First Company; had done it with zest, even lust. Now at this moment he was precious near to striking the affected fool of an officer facing him. His two comrades would back him up and in this raging snowstorm no one else could see them. Yet, he considered, didn't all this mean that he was falling into the 'trap of soldiering', which his imprisoned father had warned him about long ago? Wasn't he becoming like the rest, fighting and killing without thought, without feeling? Strike Creeping Jesus now and it would mean the end of his silent rebellion. One way or another the system would have him. He would be one of Hitler's soldiers – '*Meine geliebten*

Soldaten'* – the Führer was always enthusing about.

Karl Carstens let his shoulders slump, as if in silent defeat and said, 'Yessir. Thank you, sir.'

Behind him he heard the other two Rebels gasp at his tame submission. Karl told himself it didn't matter what they thought of him at this moment; all that mattered was what he thought about *himself*.

'Good,' Creeping Jesus went on. 'Well, as there is precious little left of the First Company to report back to, I suggest you attach yourself to *Oberfeldwebel* Bulle's kitchen platoon once more.'

'Yessir.'

'You'll find them somewhere down on the river. To the left of the old Gambsheim bridge. You know where that is, I presume?'

'Yessir,' Karl said dutifully, mind now numb, not caring what anyone thought of him.

'Good.' Creeping Jesus slapped his cane against his boot once more. 'Now then, don't just stand around. There's a war on, you know. Trot off now.'

Obediently Karl 'trotted off', followed more slowly by his two sullen and bewildered comrades. Creeping Jesus smirked at their bent backs until they finally vanished into the snowstorm. He was pleased with himself. The day had turned out well after all. He had not been forced into the combat he feared, there had been no scandal, and now the French were running for their lives in what was apparently complete disorder. The 'Poison Dwarf'** would find no difficulty in turning the night's battle into a victory for German arms; the casualties suffered by the Fourth Grenadiers would, of course, be hushed up.

Now he had just had the satisfaction of showing the impertinent Grenadier Carstens just who was master in the Fourth Grenadier Regiment. Yes, all in all, it had been a good day. Captain von Schorr slapped his boot with his cane

*'My beloved soldiers.'

**Nickname for the Nazi Minister of Propaganda Dr Josef Goebbels, on account of his size and vitriolic tongue.

once more, so pleased with himself that he hardly noticed the raging snowstorm. He had survived Poland, he told himself happily, and now undoubtedly he would survive what was to come in France. With a bit of luck, he might even convince the old fool of a CO to have him transferred to the divisional staff and then he would be able to sit out the war in absolute safety until the Führer achieved final victory, which *couldn't* be long now. For a moment Creeping Jesus indulged himself with a mental picture of a staff job in Paris, with champagne lunches and elegant French countesses who wore black silk underwear, then he shivered and remembered just how cold it was. He told himself he'd better get under cover at once. His chest was decidedly weak and he didn't want to catch a chill and be laid up when things were going so swimmingly . . .

CHAPTER 4

'DID I ever tell you two how I came to be nicknamed Ami?' The little Rhinelander broke the heavy silence as the three Rebels trudged miserably through the whirling snow, each one wrapped up in a cocoon of his own thoughts.

They didn't answer.

With weary cynicism, Ami said: 'It's nice of you to show so much enthusiasm. So I'll tell yer. My father wasn't German, yer see. He was American!'

Even Polack was roused from his leaden mood. 'An American! How come you had an American father?'

'Cos he slipped me mother a link, you big horned-ox!' Ami retorted quickly. 'Ner, because my old man was a member of the American Army during the occupation of the Rhineland. Slipped it in one dark night, slipped it out and sodded off, leaving me behind. There was a lot of us – er – bastards left when the French, English and Americans buggered off in the twenties. In the villages, where I come from, there are plenty of Jeans, Tommies and Amis like yours truly. And not only white ones either,' he added significantly.

Polack peered down at him through the snow, as if he were seeing the little Rhinelander for the first time. 'Then you ain't a real German like me and Karl?' he said.

'Real German like *you*!' Ami snorted indignantly. 'What kind o' real frigging German are you with a name like that – and an accent you could cut with a frigging knife?'

Polack wasn't offended. 'Yes, I supposed you're right, Ami. As far as I know we've allus been poor farmers in West Prussia, but there was always more Polish spoken around our village than German. Still we're classed as German.'

'Natch!' Ami snapped. 'When Adolf wants bodies, he'd even class the Grand Rabbi of Palestine as a German! Cannon fodder the Führer wants and no frigging questions asked. What do you say, Karl?'

'Suppose you're right, Ami. You know I've got a black mark against my name because my old man is an enemy of the state. What a laugh! *Enemy of the state!* My old man wouldn't have harmed a fly, but,' Karl shrugged wearily, 'he just happened to be a *sozi* who couldn't keep his big mouth shut when everybody else with any sense did. But still in spite of that I'm in the frigging Fourth Grenadiers out here in the middle of nowhere, fighting Adolf's war –'

The sound of the shot slammed into his words startlingly. Instinctively they all stumbled to a stop and peered through the snowflakes, all weariness vanished, suddenly very tense and alert. Another shot. Scarlet flame stabbed the white gloom.

'There!' Polack snapped. 'To the right – three o'clock – in them firs.'

Karl dropped to one knee and unslung his rifle hastily. The other two did the same and Ami gasped, fumbling with his safety catch. 'Are we gonna tackle them, Karl?'

Karl, his gaze fixed intently on the firs from where the firing had come, shook his head. 'Are you *meschugge*, you dumb Ami bastard? Ain't we done our share o' fighting for Adolf? From here on in, I'm declaring the three Rebels officially neutral. Except if it's our own hide or that of our comrades at stake. So just hold yer water the two of yer. Keep yer eyes peeled and let's see what's going on over there.'

'Peeled like a frigging tinned tomato!' Ami hissed and sitting back on his heels, watched his front intently, trying to penetrate the whirling white gloom.

Nearly a hundred metres away, King Bull crouched too, hardly daring to breathe, praying that his two shots had driven the black bastards off. Crying that weird shout of theirs, they had appeared frighteningly out of the snowstorm. Three of them, as black as night, almost as tall as himself, their gleaming white teeth filed to sawlike points so that they looked like coal-black sharks. For an eternity, or so it seemed, they had stared at one another in shocked silence. But he had recovered first. Ripping off two shots before they could unsling their long rifles, he had dived headlong into the firs. Madly he had scrambled for cover, burrowing ever deeper into the wood, hoping fervently that they would run on and forget him.

Now he crouched there, pistol in big hand, head cocked to one side straining to catch the slightest sound. But it was difficult. The wind howled all the time, making the firs sway alarmingly, and the snow kept slithering down from the branches at regular intervals. All the while he raged inside that this was happening to him, King Bull, master of the Fourth Grenadiers' kitchens. Why had he got to face all this danger by himself?

There was a sudden crack to his right. King Bull froze. His nostrils were assailed by a warm foreign smell. He swallowed hard. His knuckles gripping the pistol butt whitened. They hadn't moved on after all! They had come looking for him instead. He crouched even lower, not daring to move, hoping the white mantle of snow on his big shoulders would camouflage him.

Another crack. This time to his left. King Bull quailed. They were coming in from both sides. What was he going to do? *My God, why doesn't anyone come and help me?*

The noises they made came nearer. He could just imagine them creeping through the firs, baring those sawlike teeth, bayonets raised like spears, as if they were back in their native jungle stalking their prey. 'It ain't right,' he quavered to himself, 'sending in heathen savages against decent German men.' Instinctively, hardly aware that he was doing so, he started to back off, the snow slithering from him in a white rain. They'd cut the dongs off'n the peasants back in the village, hadn't they? Christ on a crutch, they'd do the same to him, if they caught him! The terrifying vision of himself with his dong cut off, leaving him with a bit of female gash, flashed before his mind's eye. He'd never have another blue-veiner! Never part that delicious beaver and dip his wick in the honey-pot! Never have a stiff'un right up under his chin, knocking the cups off'n the table every time he turned. Never –

The big black hands caught him by the throat and his nose took in the stink of garlic and cheap black tobacco. Desperately he tried to free himself from that vice-like grip. But already the others were bursting triumphantly from the firs, big scarred faces gleaming with sweat, yelling crazily; and pressed tightly to his rear he felt a familiar thickening which didn't belong to him. He gasped with shock. *They weren't going to do that to him, King Bull?* But they were. Already the other two, their yellow eyes gleaming with sexual excitement were beginning to fumble with his trousers . . .

'I can't stand it anymore, Karl!' Polack moaned and rose to his feet. 'God knows what they're doing to our lad up there. *Boshe moi*!' he cursed and clasped his hands to this ears to drown out the howls from the woods, screams that did not seem to originate from a human being, so terrible that it was as if the firs would be ripped to shreds by them.

Ami swallowed hard and rose as well. 'Do what you like, Karl, but it's awful.' He wrung his hands like a worried mother might do over a terribly sick baby. 'It's getting on my tits!'

Feeling sick and queasy, knowing however that he was being dragged into something again of which he wanted no part, Karl snapped angrily, 'All right . . . all right, don't frigging well rabbit on about it . . . And let's be shitting careful, eh? We've played heroes enough for one day.'

Reluctantly he clasped the butt of his rifle to his right hip and began to advance, half-crouched, to the sound of that terrible noise which had now given way to a soft miserable keening. Karl shivered and felt the small hairs at the back of his neck stand erect. What in three devils' name was going on in the firs?

Suddenly he stopped dead. There was one of the gigantic blacks slipping through the firs. There seemed something evil and ghost-like about him: the black bogeyman of his childhood nightmares.

'*Frog*!' Polack gasped. In one and the same movement he brought up his rifle and fired.

The Senegalese faltered in mid-stride. He gave a strange feminine, almost hysterical scream and the next instant flopped forward. Karl spun round on Polack, eyes blazing with fury. 'What did you want to go and do that for, you Polish idiot? Do you want to be a damn fucking hero –'

'*Look out, Karl!*' Ami screeched.

Karl flashed round and fired from the hip without even being conscious he was doing so. Six metres away the other Senegalese who had blundered out of the wood, long bayonet aimed directly at Karl's back, reeled back abruptly, dark red blood welling up instantly from a hole in his belly. He sat down with a hard jolt and began to cry like a spoiled child. Polack went over and kicked him in the face. He stopped crying and concentrated on holding his hands pressed tight to his wounded stomach. Otherwise his broad scarred face showed no emotion.

Ami bent down and flung his bayonet deep into the trees. 'Come on,' he said when Karl didn't move. 'Let's sort it out once and for all. I can't stand much frigging more of this, Karl.'

They moved on towards the sound of that eerie keening, leaving the dying Senegalese propped against the tree, watching their departure with emotionless eyes; as if his fate had been decided and there was no point expending unnecessary emotion on the matter . . .

'Holy strawsack!' Ami gasped and came to an abrupt stop. Polack clapped his hand to his forehead in sheer disbelief. Karl swallowed hard and stifled the sudden desire to laugh out loud just in time.

King Bull crouched on his knees, naked rump stuck in the air, staring in a dazed fashion at the ground, uttering soft moans and shaking his head at the same time, as if he could not understand the iniquity of life. Next to him, shot cleanly through the forehead by Polack and already dead, lay one of the giant Senegalese, with what looked like a good length of rubber hose in his hand - though it wasn't rubber hose.

'*Oberfeld*,' Karl said softly, wild laughter at the sight exploding in his mind. How sweet this moment was, he told himself! It was worth a month's pay.

Slowly, very slowly, King Bull turned to look up at them, eyes dazed and bewildered, as if he could not quite comprehend how he had managed to get here, alone in the middle of the snowy wood, with his trousers down and a dead negro lying beside him. He seemed shrunken too and paler than normal. 'Yes?' he asked, saliva dribbling down the side of his slack mouth. 'Yes?'

'What happened?' Karl asked in his turn, though he had already guessed what *Oberfeldwebel* Bulle had undergone. It would undoubtably be one sexual experience of which he would not boast to his cronies of the sergeants' mess. 'Did they hurt you, Sergeant?'

'Did they hurt me?' King Bull moaned and then in an attempt to recover his lost dignity, he struggled to his feet and pulled up his pants. 'Have you forgotten military regulations? he demanded, but there was none of the old fire in his voice. 'What are you supposed to do in the presence of a superior officer, greenbeak, tell me that?'

Karl looked around cheekily, as if he were searching for someone and said, as if slightly stupid. 'Senior officer? What senior officer?'

King Bull flung out his big chest, as if he were just about to explode into one of his feared rages; then he saw the looks on the young men's faces and saw the fearful apprehension which had once been reflected there was no longer present. Instead their eyes were hard and knowing and not a little contemptuous. The rage vanished as soon as it had come. Abruptly King Bull was deflated, weak, even a little comical. He fumbled awkwardly with his helmet as Karl said softly, 'Remember, you big bastard, we saved your life, and,' he hissed insidiously, 'we know what happened to you as well!'

King Bull said nothing. He turned without another word and started to stumble through the storm towards the river, ignoring the mocking laughter which followed him. But within that oddly shrunken body, his heart raged. The three of them knew what the niggers had done to him. If they opened their traps they could ruin his life – he might even lose his beloved kitchens. He clenched his fists with a sudden return of his spirits, as he came to that overwhelming decison. *The three of them would have to die . . !*

CHAPTER 5

NOW AS the battle raged back and forth in Norway and the planners in Berlin worked feverishly on the attack to come in France – for now it had been postponed to May – the Western Front settled down once more. Under the temporary command of Captain von Schorr while the CO recovered, the battered Fourth Grenadiers took in replacements daily. Chased out of the trucks by the red-faced NCOs, given the command to sing, '*one, two, three – a song* –' they would march proudly through the gates of the *Adolf Hitler Kaserne* to be met by Creeping Jesus and the NCO Corps.

'We train hard in the Fourth Grenadiers,' he would rasp in that weak silly voice of his, slapping his gleaming boot all the time with his cane, 'and fight easy! We have no time for weaklings here. As the Führer has said,' and his face would take on a look of awed respect at the mention of Hitler's name, ' "we must be as speedy as the greyhound, as tough as old leather and as bold as the lion." Sarnt-Major – *wheel 'em away*!'

And they would be duly 'wheeled away' by the hard-faced cynical NCOs to day after day of back-breaking brutal exercises, constantly chivvied and cried at by the sergeants who were here, there and everywhere, like savage dogs barking at the heels of dumb sheep. 'Use the frigging butt, you piss-pansy – *smash his frigging skull in, willya*! Turn the blade when yer thrusts it into the frog's guts and if it won't come *pump a slug into him and blow yersen free! Rip open his jugular vein . . . Grabs hold of his balls, yer do and twists them like this . . . till his frigging eyes pop . . .'*

On and on it went as winter gave way to the spring of 1940, the greatest year in the history of Hitler's vaunted 'One Thousand Year Reich', with those bruised, sweating, frightened young men slowly being brutalized, turned into the toughest, most professional soldiers the world had ever known.

All this training passed by the three Rebels. Yet once again they were on permanent fatigues in King Bull's kitchens, as if the Fourth Grenadiers had forgotten them and they would spend *their* war washing-up; though Karl had a shrewd suspicion both Creeping Jesus and King Bull preferred to have them out of the way.

While outside the snow gave way to rain and then the balmy days of a beautiful April, the three comrades toiled in the kitchens, surrounded by the constant clatter of pans, the hiss of steam, the fierce chatter of the gas jets. Bread was handled by the hundredweight, coffee came in fountains, eggs by the hundred dozen. Potatoes were hauled by the hundred pound and peeled in a clattering rotating machine the size of a concrete mixer. Cooks climbed steel ladders to taste the soups bubbling away in massive cauldrons. Lettuces were docked like captives' heads by cooks wielding cleavers that hissed through the air like executioners' axes . . .

And all the while Karl, Polack and Ami scraped, washed and rinsed, trying to beat the relentless pile after pile of dirty dishes, hour after hour, day after day, week after week until their every pore stank of the rotting muckiness of food waste. Still they did not complain. As Ami was wont to remark, 'Better pearl-diving any day, comrades, than watching the taties grow – *from two metres below*!' It was a sentiment with which the other two agreed wholeheartedly, especially now as King Bull had been tamed, or so it seemed; for he rarely inspected their corner of the huge, echoing kitchens and even when he did he remained glum and silent. Yet occasionally Karl had chanced on him staring at them, his big brick-red face thoughtful, his little eyes red and hard, fists clenched, as if he were managing to restrain himself only by a sheer effort of willpower. At such moments, Karl felt an uneasy sensation of apprehension: a feeling of disquiet, wondering what might be going on in that big cropped head.

In that first week of April, the three Rebels had the first indication that King Bull had recovered his nerve and that he was back to his old tricks, attempting to make 'scarlet sows' of them; to what purpose they did not know. It was a Wednesday, traditionally 'fart soup and sausage day'. The air in the hot kitchen was heavy with the smell of peas and the cooks went about their work, farting at regular intervals with the usual dramatic calls for 'deep silence, comrades, I have an important announcement for you!' before lifting one haunch and gleefully ripping off a great burst of wind. But on this particular 'fart soup and sausage day', there was a difference, though the three Rebels wreathed in steam at their great sinks did not notice it till afterwards: the cooks winked constantly at each other, sly looks on their fat pale faces, as if they were sharing some secret or other. King Bull had returned to his usual boastful swagger, too, bellowing his orders across the noisy kitchen and once even shrilling a blast on that silver whistle which had caused so much fear among fatigue men in the old days.

Now as the last of the 'dinner-men' started to leave the cookhouse, stomachs swollen with pea soup, picking at their teeth with matchsticks, the pots and pans kept piling up in front of the three sweating Rebels, puzzlingly. Up to his hairy elbows in greasy water, great beads of glistening sweat hanging from his black bushy eyebrows, Polack swore in Polish and exclaimed: 'Never in my frigging life have I seen those hash-slingers use so many frigging pots and pans! What do they think this is – the Führer's wedding party or something?'

'You know that our beloved Führer has no time for such things as sex and marriage,' Ami quipped, scraping at the hard green-crusted walls of the soup dixies. 'His whole life is devoted to his beloved folk-comrades!'

But by two o'clock with the piles of pans mounting ever more in front of them so that they were no longer able to see the cooks' grinning, knowing faces, even Ami's sense of humour had vanished. Like the rest he concentrated solely on trying to cope with this monstrous washing-up, the like of which they had never encountered before in all their months in King Bull's celebrated kitchen.

It was only at three-thirty, with the pans still growing in the steaming troughs, although the cooks had long ago finished with their preparations for *Abendbrot** that they noticed something was wrong. Almost casually, twirling his silver whistle, King Bull strolled over to them and remarked, 'Bit slow on those pans, Grenadiers. Should have been finished by now. Doesn't look as if you're gonna get much of a break before evening meal, does it, Carstens? You'll have to work straight through, probably.'

Karl wiped the sweat from his brick-red, lathered face with the back of his wrist and stared at the big noncom, a look of unconcealed triumph on his ugly mug, and said, 'I suppose I'm just slow, *Oberfeld*.'

'The night shift'll need them pans, too. Can't see you lot getting into bed with the old one-handed widow for a bit of you know what before lights out this day.' He guffawed hugely and made an obscene gesture with his clenched right fist.

Karl's face grew crimson. 'I allus, thought, *Oberfeld*, that a good cook never uses more pans than he needs to. A good cook saves his fatigue men work.'

King Bull shrugged easily. 'So I hear. Perhaps I'm surrounded by plain frigging bad cooks. Anyhow let's knock off the moaning and get on with the job, eh, Grenadiers? Report to me just before lights out if you've got any complaints. I'll give you a tough shit chitty to take to the padre!' He sniggered and strolled away, followed by the admiring looks of his cooks, who knew that this day the head cook had successfully made the three Rebels into 'scarlet sows'.

That incident of 'fart soup and sausage day' marked the start of King Bull's efforts to restore his deflated ego and pride by a systematic campaign of harassment and humiliation against the three Rebels.

*Supper.

Now, aided by the fawning cooks, King Bull piled up the work so much that it was rare that the three of them finished their duties before ten at night. Breaks vanished. Even the very food they ate had to be swallowed at the double. Not that their stomachs, even Polack's, could tolerate much of it. For now they were persistently nauseated and made queasy by the unremitting routine of 'pearl-diving' in the scummy sinks from morning to night. Slowly the three of them began to realize what King Bull's plan was. They formed an ever-present danger to him. He wanted them to commit such a gross act of disobedience that they would be sent off to Torgau for good.

'The prime prick is needling us, comrades,' Ami announced one night as they lay in their bunks unable to get to sleep in spite of their exhaustion, because Polack had the 'hot heaves' (as they called vomiting) yet once again. 'King Bull's kitchens ain't such a safe billet as we thought they was. Sooner or later he'll catch us with our drawers down – and then he'll really saw off our asses!'

Lying there in the gloom, hands under his head, disgusted with his own stink, which no amount of washing with ersatz *kernseife** could eradicate, Karl told himself Ami was right. King Bull was needling them into a situation from which there would be no escape . . .

Two days later, King Bull took them off the sinks personally.

'You lucky lot!' he announced, leading them away from the piles of dirty dishes and pans, to one of the long halls which fed the stores into the kitchen. 'The officers' mess is throwing a chicken dinner and I thought you'd like a change.' He flung out a big paw like a head waiter ushering a favoured client to his table. 'There you are, lads. Get that little lot cleaned and dressed and the rest of the day is yours. Now don't thank me for my generosity, just get cracking. The

*A kind of liquid soap.

mess steward wants them by four this evening.' And with that he was gone, leaving them to stare in bewilderment at his broad back.

For a few moments they looked at the barrels which lined the one side of the room and then Polack took out his knife, inserted it under the lid of the first one, and heaved. He blanched. The barrel was filled to the top with chickens, naked and yellow, replete with heads and feet.

Karl looked over his shoulder and spat on the floor in disgust. 'The bastard!' he hissed. 'Look at 'em. We've got to take off the heads, the feet, and then clean out the guts. There's enough work there for a whole shitting platoon, never mind the three of us, if we're gonna get them done by four!'

'Yer know his frigging game, don't yer?' Ami said, staring in dismay at the barrels of chickens. 'He's gone and told the mess steward they'll be ready for four, although he knows we can't make it by then. The mess steward has reported the same to Creeping Jesus and when we don't make it, the shit'll hit the fan; and who'll be at the receiving end of the ordour? – *Us*! Creeping Jesus'll come down on us like a heap of bricks. Buy combs, comrades,' he ended sombrely, 'for there's lousy times ahead!'

'Cut the shitting cackle!' Polack snapped urgently. 'I for one am not gonna give the big bastard the pleasure of landing me behind Swedish curtains.* Let's get on with it.' He reached into the barrel, pulled out one of the chickens and with a swift gesture split it open. Awkwardly he pulled out gizzard, craw, liver and heart and then reached for his knife to slice off the claws, with hands that were already greasy and covered with gore. Even as he did so, the knife slipped from his grip and tumbled to the table.

Karl grabbed at it before Polack could reach it. 'No, that's not the way,' he snapped. 'You'll be slicing off more of your own pinkies than chicken feet in the end. We've got to organize this like a factory production belt. You split 'em, Polack, you've got the right paws for a job like that. You cut

*Army slang for prison bars.

out the guts, Ami, and I'll rinse 'em and stack 'em. Now come on, let's get organized.'

Thus while outside total war raged, the *Battle of the Chicken Production Line*, as Karl would call it after their victory over King Bull, commenced: a battle waged just as much for self-respect, justice and democracy as any the Western Allies fought that spring nearly fifty years ago now . . .

CHAPTER 6

NOW THEY sweated out the four o'clock deadline. On one side of the metal table, Polack pulled the chickens out of the barrels, ripped them apart with one powerful tug and opened their vents. Instantly he pushed the sticky yellow carcass to Ami on the other side, who pulled out guts, giblets, gizzard and craw, pushed the liver and heart, which the cooks would use, to one side, before shoving the bird to a waiting Karl. He whipped his cleaver down to sever feet and head, split the breasts in two, rinsed them and flung them into the waiting tray.

At first they talked, but after the first hour, they found they had neither the time nor the energy for chatter. Instead they concentrated on their grisly task with one hundred per cent effort. By the end of the second hour, they were gasping like men running a long strenuous race, their arms glistening with red gore, knee-deep in the remains of chicken, the air about them heavy with the cloying stench of dead birds.

At midday King Bull sauntered in, apparently casually, his piglike red eyes taking in the scene with obvious pleasure: the sweat-lathered, blood-stained young men, tearing, tugging, slicing, severing the carcasses like automatons, with, in the corner, the many barrels of chicken still untouched.

'Suppose you should have a break for dinner,' he said and flicked the ash from his cigar into the tray piled high with chicken breast. 'But I guess you'll want to get the job done with so you can break off early.' He turned to go and then stopped to say casually, 'Oh, and by the way, the Adjutant himself is very concerned that the job is done on time. Apparently the divisional commander is coming to dinner in the officers' mess. It's gonna be a big do, white wine and finger bowls for the general to dip his pinkies into. Better not be late, Grenadiers.' And with that he went out again, an ugly grin on his big face.

'Arse with ears!' Ami cursed not stopping his slicing for one moment.

Polack grunted and tore another carcass open, as if he might well have been ripping open King Bull's rib-cage, while Karl gasped, 'Those Senegalese should have stuffed him so much that his frigging eyes popped out!'

By two that afternoon, they were swaying on their feet, sickened by the stink of all that dead flesh, their hands cold and white-wrinkled from reaching into so many chickens' guts. Now their distaste and tiredness after six hours of cleaning the damned birds began to turn into anger and rage at a world which forced them to do such things.

Once Ami's knife slipped and he yelped with pain as he cut into his forefinger. Exasperated beyond measure, he picked up the blood-stained chicken and flung it in sudden fury against the opposite wall. 'Frigging chickens!' he cursed. 'Why did God create the rotten things? All they do is lay frigging eggs!'

Five minutes later Polack ripped open another bird and recoiled as something particularly bloody, stinking, and highly unpleasant fell into his big hands. In that same instant one of the cooks came in, jeering, 'Not finished yet, you –'

Polack flung the chicken at him and he went reeling back, blood running down his cheeks where the dead bird's beak had broken the flesh. 'I'll report you to King Bull!' he cried. 'Fancy being hurt by a frigging dead chicken! I'll report you –'

Polack raised another chicken threateningly. The injured cook fled. Doggedly they worked on, their hands slick with the slime from the dead birds, hating their waxy yellow skin, hating King Bull, the Army, the whole *damned rotten world*!

At three Ami began to puke helplessly into one of the empty chicken barrels, skinny shoulders heaving as if he were sobbing. Bravely he continued his work, vomiting into the barrel and then ripping out yet another birds' entrails with a hand that shook violently. King Bull wandered in casually, carrying a canteen of coffee, obviously well-laced with cognac. He took a sip of the steaming hot brew, smacking his lips with appreciation. 'Nothing can beat a cup of good ole nigger sweat, with a good shot of sauce in it, can it?' he declared.

The whiff of *Kognak* set Ami off again. He turned from the table and retched miserably into the barrel, sobbing for breath.

King Bull smiled easily. 'You got a delicate stomach, Grenadier Doepgen?' he sneered. 'Should have thought it would have taken more than a bit o' chicken guts to turn the stomach of a hero like you.' He made a great play of looking at the filled barrels and then at his watch, before announcing, 'Not much more time left. Fifty minutes to go . . . and I *did* promise, the Adje . . . 'Fraid he's gonna burn your asses for this one, men.' He grinned at them maliciously and sauntered out sipping his 'nigger sweat'.

Karl flung down his knife, eyes blazing with fury. 'That does it!' he declared. 'I will not dress another shitting chicken!'

Ami did the same and hung on to the edge of the table, sobbing for breath like a man who had just run a great race. Only Polack held on to his blood-stained carcass, saying, 'But if we don't finish 'em by four, Karl, then they've got us. We'll be right up to our hooters in crap! They'll have us inside the guardroom in zero, comma, nothing seconds!'

Karl nodded, eyes flashing fire. 'I know, I know, Polack. But there must be a way to screw 'em. *There must!*'

For a few moments there was a heavy silence in the stinking room, broken only by the hiss of steam from the urns outside, while Karl thought and the other two eyed him anxiously, expectantly. Slowly, very slowly, Karl's bloodshot eyes began to light up, as the idea started to take shape in his mind. Ami bit his bottom lip. Polack licked his lips. Was there going to be a way out? Could Karl, the brightest of the three Rebels, swing it? Polack, the farmboy, told himself Karl had gone to school in the big city; he knew all sorts of tricks that he, Polack, had never even dreamed of. He waited with bated breath.

'We've been idiots all the time,' Karl said slowly, almost as if he were talking to himself. 'We've been letting that big bastard King Bull run the show, just tamely taking the kind of crap he's been flinging at us . . .'

'What do you mean, Karl?' Ami asked.

Karl didn't seem to hear. Instead he continued in his slow thoughtful manner, as if he were formulating his plans as he talked. 'King Bull commands and we obey . . . like a lot of frigging sheep being led to the slaughter! But it doesn't have to be that way.' Suddenly his worn face was animated by new energy, the adrenaline pumping fire into his bloodstream. 'Listen,' he announced, 'how many full barrels have we got left?'

Miserably Polack replied, 'Five – and we'll never finish *them* by four, Karl.'

'Oh yes, we will,' Karl said triumphantly.

'But how?' Polack protested plaintively.

'Because we're not going to dress the frigging awful things, that's how . . . Polack, take this cleaver.' He flung the bloodstained hatchet and the big Rebel caught it – just. 'Get cracking and start pulling the floorboards up – there in the corner. Don't ask questions, we've only got twenty minutes or so left!'

Big face completely bewildered, Polack started to do as he was told, while Karl turned to Ami and barked, 'Come on, gimme a hand to unload these crappy chickens. *I'm gonna show you how to dress five barrels of our frigging feathered friends in five minutes flat . . .'*

King Bull came to a sudden halt.

The three Rebels, hands and faces washed and scrubbed, sat on their stools, calmly puffing at their cigarettes, next to the huge pile of trays containing chicken breasts. He gasped. But it wasn't the fact that the three fatigue men were actually daring to *smoke* in his kitchens that made him gasp. He stared in disbelief at the empty chicken barrels. 'You've . . . finished 'em,' he croaked, twisting his head to one side like a man being strangled. 'You've finished 'em . . . and it's not even four o'clock . . .'

Karl nodded. Casually he flicked his ash onto the giblet-strewn floor.

'But . . . how did you do it?' King Bull croaked, too surprised to be angry at the way his beloved kitchens were being desecrated. 'I didn't think it was poss –'

'Just plain old hard work, *Oberfeld*.' Karl cut him short.

Next to him, Ami repressed his laughter with difficulty. Even Polack's sombre slavic features were fringed with a smile.

Blindly King Bull stumbled by them to the barrels. He stuck his hand in each one, feeling the interior, as if he simply could not believe that they had actually emptied them. But they had. There was not a single chicken carcass left to be dressed. He stood up finally, shaking his head in sheer absolute bewilderment.

Slowly Karl rose to his feet and calmly stubbed out his cigarette on the slime-covered table. 'Four o'clock,' he announced, while King Bull stared at him, mouth open like a village idiot. 'You said, "Get that little lot cleaned and dressed and the rest of the day's yours." We've done it. Come on, comrades, give the *Oberfeld* a salute* and let's be on our way. I'm looking forward to an early night for a change.' Sloppily the three saluted the big head cook and strolled out of the kitchen, stared at by the amazed cooks.

'But what about this mess . . . the slime, the carcasses?' a dazed King Bull called from behind them.

Karl didn't look back. Airily he cried, 'Sorry about that, *Oberfeld*. Our time's up. But some of these cooks here seem to have nothing much to do . . .' They sauntered outside into the fresh spring afternoon whistling cheerfully.

That night, the *Adolf Hitler Kaserne* was heavy with the smell of fried chicken and it came not only from the *Kasino***, where the elegantly uniformed grenadier officers wined and dined

*In the German Army, NCOs were saluted from the rank of corporal upwards.
**Officers' mess.

with the divisional commander, General-Major von Udet. In virtually every barrack room occupied by the various drafts there was a chicken frying merrily on the coal stoves, eager young men licking their lips in anticipation of the treat to come; after all, for most of them chicken was a delicacy they ate only once a year, at Christmas.

Only Karl, Ami and Polack did not participate in the illicit feast they had provided for their young comrades. They had had enough chicken to last them a lifetime. Instead they squatted on the stoop outside their blacked-out barracks room, drinking the beer from the big two litre jug which a grateful platoon had bought them in return for the chickens, chatting happily, enjoying their first lazy evening for months. 'If only the big prick had known he was standing on top of five barrels' worth of chicken!' Ami said and belched pleasurably. 'Holy strawsack, he would have flipped his wig!'

Polack nodded his agreement happily.

'I nearly flipped *my* wig when those fatigue men started coming out, with our feathered friends hidden under their fatigues,' Karl said and took another drink of beer from his canteen. 'If King Bull had cottoned on, he would really have zapped our asses. Insubordination, stealing *Wehrmacht* property, incitement to theft – the whole lot!'

'But he didn't, did he?' Polack growled and stared across at the *Kasino*, from where now came the sound of a Strauss waltz played by the Grenadiers' regimental band. 'Do you think the gentlemen officers dance with each other?' he asked, a little drunk, then hiccuped.

'Idiot!' Karl snapped. 'Though I don't know,' he added after a moment's thought. 'A lot of 'em do look like shitting warm brothers*. But to be serious, comrades. This is the last time that King Bull – the big prick – ever pulls a trick like that with the chickens on us. From here on in, *we fight back*!'

Carried away by the beauty of the spring night, the beer, a sudden heady excitement, as he recalled how they had

*German slang for homosexual.

tricked the head cook, Karl raised his canteen. 'Comrades, Rebels,' he said solemnly, 'I give you a toast.'

Ami and Polack raised their canteens, too.

'War to the death against King Bull and all his hash-slingers!' Karl cried fervently. *'Prost!'*

'War to the death against King Bull and all his hash-slingers! Prost!' Ami and Polack growled in unison. They touched canteens, drained them and next instant doubled up with crazy drunken laughter, three happy young men enjoying this time out of war in the spring of 1940 . . .

Fifty metres away, while the Grenadiers' band scrapped through 'Wienerblut', red-faced, corseted General von Udet thrust back his chair and rose to his feet to propose a toast too. With his well-manicured hand, the nails of which were delicately tinted a light red, he tapped his spoon against his glass and called, '*Meine Herren.*'

Creeping Jesus, seated to his right in the place of honour, cleared his throat and glared at the wine-flushed officers seated around the long table with its gleaming white damask table-cloth.

The chatter subsided and, adjusting his monocle, the divisional commander stared around at their faces to announce, 'Gentlemen, we have a date!'

Someone gasped. A young subaltern sprang to his feet with excitement and then realizing that everyone was looking at him, sat down again abruptly. Creeping Jesus swallowed hard, that old familiar fear overcoming him again like an icy-cold wave.

'You will all be glad to know,' the general went on, pleased with the effect of his surprise, 'that we will march westwards before the month of May is out . . . *Please, please*, hear me out! The Fourth Grenadiers will have its old objective. Undoubtedly it will be a bloody business, a very bloody business indeed and your chaps will have to pay the butcher's bill . . . But it will bring glory to the old regiment to which I once belonged.' He raised his glass level with the third button of his tunic, elbow extended at a forty-five degree angle as military regulations prescribed. '*Meine Herren*, I will give you a toast.'

As one they thrust back their chairs and rose to their feet, glasses poised.

'Gentlemen, to the honour of the regiment - and victory in the west!' he rasped in his high-pitched nasal voice. *'Prosit!'*

'To the honour of the regiment - and victory in the west!' half a hundred voices cried as one. *'Prosit!'* Next moment the glasses started to fly at the wall to explode in a flurry of broken glass and instinctively the band of the Grenadiers burst into that bombastic anthem which soon the whole of Europe would fear, 'Deutschland ueber Alles . . .'

CHAPTER 7

'*FIGHT TERROR with terror*,' now became the motto of the three Rebels, as April passed and the *Wehrmacht* massed all along Germany's frontier with France, readying for the great attack westwards.

There was, for example, the incident of the 'gigantic black rat, foaming at the mouth', which haunted King Bull's kitchens for a week and reduced his cooks to gibbering terror.

In fact, the 'gigantic black rat' was a stray cat, which the Rebels smuggled into the kitchens one late afternoon while most of the cooks were taking their nap. With Polack guarding the door, the other two let it loose. It was a feast day for the half-starved stray. It sprang from one delicacy to another, scratching here, biting there, licking over there, leaving behind it a trail of sausage skins, clawed chickens and half-eaten chocolate strewn all over the kitchens for the sleepy cooks to find when they came down to prepare the evening meal. 'It was a rat, *Herr Obergefreiter*,' Polack reported in that slow peasant manner of his when a waxen-faced Corporal Tietze asked. 'Biggest I've ever seen, even back on the farm. This big –' He extended his hands to depict the creature's size and Tietze shuddered dramatically – 'and he slipped down there, just as I flung the frigging cleaver at him!' He indicated the hole in the floor and the cleaver lying next to it.

Naturally King Bull was summoned. '*A rat in my kitchen*!' he exploded. 'It's not possible. I won't allow it. My God, what if the Adjutant ever found out . . . Set traps . . . set traps everywhere . . .'

But with the cunning of its kind, the 'gigantic black rat', which had now actually been seen by one of the cooks who described it as 'foaming at the mouth', managed to avoid all attempts at capture. Every afternoon it wreaked havoc in King Bull's immaculate kitchens and then disappeared under the floorboards for the rest of the day. For a week the gleeful Rebels kept up the hoax, but when in the end an irate King Bull started to post cooks armed with rifles and cleavers at all possible exits for the elusive rodent, they decided they had gone far enough. The obliging stray cat, which had now attached itself to them, brought in a skinny mouse it had found somewhere or other one afternoon and Karl draped its broken little body in one of the traps dramatically.

'And that's what you call a frigging gigantic black rat, Tietze!' King Bull exploded when he saw it, 'foaming at the frigging mouth! *You* ought to be foaming at the frigging mouth . . . Now get it out of my kitchens toot-sweet!' And the head cook turned and marched away, muttering to himself in disgust, leaving the cooks to stare at the 'monster' which had terrorized them all week.

Soon after that there was the business of King Bull's 'private pig'. King Bull had received the Adjutant's permission to feed the kitchen waste to the pig which he had purchased from one of the local farmers. 'Of course, *Herr Hauptmann*, there will be a prime cut of pork for you, sir, once I kill it,' he assured Creeping Jesus. 'Or if you wish it, sir,' he had lowered his voice conspiratorially, 'I know a certain gent who is prepared to pay a good price for a nice piece of pork.' He winked knowingly and departed with the Adjutant's good wishes.

Now the pink pig was fattened daily on the carefully selected waste King Bull had the fatigue men feed it in the cage he had had built for it, right next to his own quarters. Indeed so proud was King Bull of his pig, which one day would bring him a tidy sum on the black market, that he weighed it daily and marked up the figure on a slate attached to the sty. It was rumoured, too, in the kitchens that he kept a gun handy next to his bed, in case some intruder attempted to steal his prize animal, to which he had now given the name of his current mistress, 'Gerda'.

'Well, that's understandable enough,' Ami commented when he heard the news. 'Both of 'em have got the same ugly mug. Only the pig's arse is prettier!'

Karl appeared not to hear, as he pondered how he might deprive King Bull of the money he would one day earn with his 'Gerda'. 'Of course, we could nick it,' he said, thinking aloud.

'*City slicker*!' Polack growled. 'Have you ever tried to move a pig which don't want to be moved? What a racket they kick up - and I for one don't fancy the big bastard taking potshots at my *derrière* with that pistol of his!'

'Yer,' Ami chimed in, cleaning his fingernails with a kitchen fork, as they waited for the evening rush to commence. 'Even if you could get fat Gerda out of her sty without King Bull noticing, how you gonna manage passing her through the sentries at the gate, that is if you want to flog her on the black market, eh?'

'I'll think about it,' was Karl's answer . . .

But while Karl pondered the abduction of 'Gerda', King Bull did some earnest thinking too. Journeying to and fro on his black market trips in the Red Zone, he saw the military build-up taking place everywhere. On all sides, the roads, the lanes, the fields were packed with shell dumps, petrol depots and tanks squatting like grey bugs under their camouflage netting. Troops were everywhere, packing each village and hamlet; there was not a single barn the whole length of the Rhine which did not house troops. Panzermen in their smart black uniforms, the flyboys of the *Luftwaffe* in their dove-grey, and the field-grey of the infantry, the 'stubble-hoppers', were packed into every available house, cottage, barn, church-hall in their thousands, and hundreds of thousands.

The *Sitzkrieg** was over, King Bull told himself morosely more than once. Soon the *Wehrmacht* would be going into action again, and although the frogs were a degenerate lot who made love with their mouths, as everyone knew, they were still dug in behind a metre of reinforced concrete on the other side of the Rhine. Syphilitic pricks they might well be, all the same they could shoot a man dead from within those fortresses

*The 'sitting war', the 'phoney war' as the inactivity on the Western Front was called cynically in 1939/40.

of theirs – and King Bull had no intention of being one of those killed in the coming offensive.

But he knew that old fool of a CO of theirs, Colonel von Heinersdorff, had returned to the regiment and was breathing fire once more, impatient for action and some desperate glory. And King Bull wanted no repetition of Bzura when the old prick had thrown in clerks and cooks, everybody. He shuddered, as he thought, too, of what the Senegalese had done to him in the woods.

So what was he going to do? How was he going to avoid the action soon to come? It was roughly the same time Karl solved the problem of how he was going to abduct 'Gerda' that King Bull came up with the solution of how he might dodge the coming battle.

'Of course!' he exclaimed, as the brilliant idea came to him with the total revelation of a vision. 'That's it. I've got it!' He thrust his naked loins closer to Gerda's, who happened to be under him at the time.

'*Oooooh*!' the plump burgomaster's daughter sighed with delight.

'My old man told me about them in the First World War . . . I think there's even one left in the regimental museum!' he yelled excitedly and thrust even harder.

'*OOOOHHHHHH*!' Gerda shuddered and moaned in ecstasy, the bed squeaking frantically, her face flushed, contorted and ugly, eyes pressed tightly together. *'Sock it to me, Schatzi . . !'*

'The old man said they'd fed from it all the way from Aachen to the frog coast . . . My God, it's the way out . . .'

Gerda opened her eyes wildly and cried desperately, breasts wobbling like jellies with absolute, unrestrained passion, 'Oh no, *Schatzi*, please don't take it *OUT* . . .'

'Out you go, Polack!' Karl standing by the door of the blacked-out barracks hissed.

Hurriedly Polack wheeled the stolen pram into the square, while Ami, still angry and embarrassed at the role he was going to play in the abduction of 'Gerda', adjusted the borrowed dress.

Karl took one final look to left and right – the square was deserted – and then, picking up the litre bottle of schnaps, liberally doctored with sugar stolen from the kitchen, followed. Somewhere a clock chimed *One . . . two . . . three.* The strokes echoed hollowly back and forth across the barracks, bathed in the silver light of a spectral moon. Karl told himself in two hours' time it would be first light. By then the abduction would have to be completed, for the fat taxi-driver, who was their new contact with the black market, had sworn he would wait only ten minutes at the most outside the gate of the *Adolf Hitler Kaserne* for 'Gerda'.

Carefully, Polack praying that the wheels of the ancient wickerwork pram would not squeak, they crossed the empty square heading for King Bull's quarters. Now they could smell 'Gerda' and hear her contented snoring, the product of a couple of litres of prime kitchen waste.

'*Himmel, Arsch und Wolkenbruch*,' Ami cursed, 'if anyone could see us now! Polack with the pram and me in this frigging dress. Like a frigging warm brothers' wedding!'

'I think you're ravishing,' Karl simpered and ducked as a disgusted Ami aimed a punch at his head.

Now they could see the sty and Gerda's first faint stirring as she began to awake, alerted by the strange noise.

Polack touched his finger to his lips. 'Leave her to me,' he warned. 'Hogs are temperamental animals. You've got to treat 'em careful or they kick up a helluva racket, just like geese.' He relinquished his hold of the pram. 'Gimme the firewater, Karl,' he ordered.

Obediently Karl handed the bottle of laced schnaps over. Polack unscrewed the cap, took a deep swig, grunted with pleasure and then advanced on a suddenly suspicious 'Gerda', face all sweetness and light, grunting softly. '*Nug . . . nug . . . nug*,' he mimicked, holding the bottle ready. 'Come on, dear Gerda . . . Come to old Polack . . . *nug, nug . . . nug . . .*'

The sow stirred restlessly in the straw. Karl tensed. Next to him Ami in his floral dress clutched his arm like a nervous woman. If they were rumbled it would mean Torgau Military Prison, that was certain.

Suddenly Polack dived forward. In one and the same moment, acting with surprising speed for such a big man, he grabbed 'Gerda' by the snout, thrust it open and in the next instant had inserted the bottle and forced the beast's head back.

'Gerda' made a stifled grunt and twisted her plump little body so that Polack had to use all his strength not to lose his grip on her and then – *wonderfully* – she began to guzzle the potent mixture, her curly little tail wiggling with delight. The abduction of Gerda had commenced . . .

'*Wer da*?' the young sentry demanded, springing out of his sentry box, rifle levelled at the strange couple pushing the pram who had suddenly appeared out of the silver darkness.

'Who do you frigging think – *Zarah Leander?*'* Karl growled.

'Tut-tut,' Ami, hanging on Karl's arm, simpered. 'My dear husband, you must watch your language, especially in the presence of the child.' Ami reached out and tenderly patted the bundle inside the pram Karl was pushing.

The young sentry, one of the most recent draft to the Fourth Grenadiers, looked puzzled. Karl could read his mind. He was asking himself what was a woman and child and a private soldier doing out at this time of the morning. In a minute he would say he was going to call the guard commander, probably some hairy-assed old vet, who would rumble them immediately.

'Conjugal visit,' Karl said firmly, and added, 'Wifey darling, don't forget baby's bottle.'

'Conjugal visit?' the sentry echoed puzzled.

'Yer, have you got plush-ears? Don't you know that we married men get a monthly chance of . . .' he leaned forward

*A well-known German film actress of the time.

and whispered something in the sentry's ear, while Ami fed the baby its bottle, eyes demurely cast on the pram, as if embarrassed by whatever Karl was relating to the sentry.

'Oh, I didn't know that,' the sentry stuttered, embarrassed himself. 'It wasn't on standing orders. Must be awkward . . . I mean . . . with all the other men in the same room.'

Karl shook his head. 'There's a special room for it in the medical centre,' he said. 'See standing orders under, "Fornication, Fathering and Fatherland".' He grabbed Ami's arm again and forced him forward. 'Come on, my little cheetah, you must not miss your taxi. Baby has his next feed in an hour . . .' Thus they passed through the gate, leaving the bewildered sentry staring after them muttering, 'See regulation "Fornication, Fathering and Fatherland",' and wondering at the strong odour of schnaps coming from the pram.

Five minutes later, Ami and Karl were tugging and heaving at a completely smashed Gerda, while the fat black-marketeer counted out his greasy *Reichsmark* notes . . .

CHAPTER 8

SURPRISINGLY ENOUGH King Bull was not too upset at the loss of his treasured pig. Admittedly he raged a little the next morning when Gerda's disappearance was discovered, raced around the kitchens sniffing everywhere for any trace of illicit cooked pork, toured the barracks with the Adjutant probing under beds and into lockers. But in the end he gave up and to the disappointment of the three Rebels, their wallets well stuffed with black market money now, never mentioned the disappearance again. 'I knew he didn't really love her,' Ami commented with his tongue in this cheek. 'And she was such a sweet little thing!' he added with a sigh. 'Imagine her all strung up in sausages, her cute little arse already blackening in somebody's smoke room, some fat civvie tucking into her chops.' He sighed again.

'*Schnauze*,' Polack grunted, 'or yer'll have me crying in me beer. All the same I'd like to know why the big bastard took it so easy.' His eyes narrowed. 'Wonder what his frigging game is?'

Karl tugged at the end of his nose, puzzled too. 'Yer, it is a bit funny. And what's he doing all the time, over at the regimental carpentry shop? As soon as the meals are over and done with, off he scoots over there every day, as if his frigging life depended upon it. He's up to something, if I know old King Bull, that he is.'

Ami dismissed the head cook and his mysterious activities. 'Come on, comrades, leave him to it.' He tapped his tunic pocket where his now bulging wallet rested and said, 'Tonight we celebrate poor old Gerda's passing.' He clutched his crotch melodramatically, 'I've got so much ink in my fountain pen, I don't know who to write to first!'

Laughing happily the three of them walked back to the barracks, leaving King Bull to his plans whatever they might be . . .

While King Bull laid his own plans for the battle soon to come, the staff of the Fourth Grenadier Regiment also prepared for the great offensive the Führer had ordered in the west. Overnight, assault boats appeared mysteriously in the *Adolf Hitler Kaserne*. One morning just before dawn the grenadiers were awakened by the clatter of tank tracks and, half-asleep, they peered out of barrack windows to spot a column of Mark IIIs which had used the cover of darkness to drive to the *Kaserne* from the nearest rail-head. A day later two bridge-building tanks, strange-looking devices which rolled a primitive bridge in front of them to span ditches and dykes, followed them. Day after day, more and more equipment made its appearance, as dispatch riders, bearing mysterious-looking pouches, roared back and forth from divisional headquarters, and staff officers, with briefcases chained to their wrists, came ever more frequently to von Heinersdorff's HQ. Rumours – 'latrine-o-grams' the old hares called them – were rife. Each dawn, as the men squatted side by side in the long line of thunderboxes, straining and moaning, there was a fresh crop of them, each one wilder than the others. But all of these rumours had one thing in common: *whatever else happened, it was certain that the Fourth Grenadier Regiment was going to make an assault crossing of the Rhine!*

'*Meine Herren*!' Colonel von Heinersdorff drew back the curtain covering the map on the wall. 'Objective . . . the French Maginot Line defensive position, Fort de Gambsheim.'

An excited rippled of sound ran through his audience in the heavily guarded map room, which he silenced with his upraised sword.

This is the latest detailed diagram, the result of months of work by Intelligence and our agents and sympathisers on the other side of the Rhine, gentlemen. Mark it well, for in the near future all of you will be seeing Fort de Gambsheim, hm, in the flesh, or would naked concrete be a better expression. Haw, haw,' he guffawed.

No one joined in. They were all too awed by what they

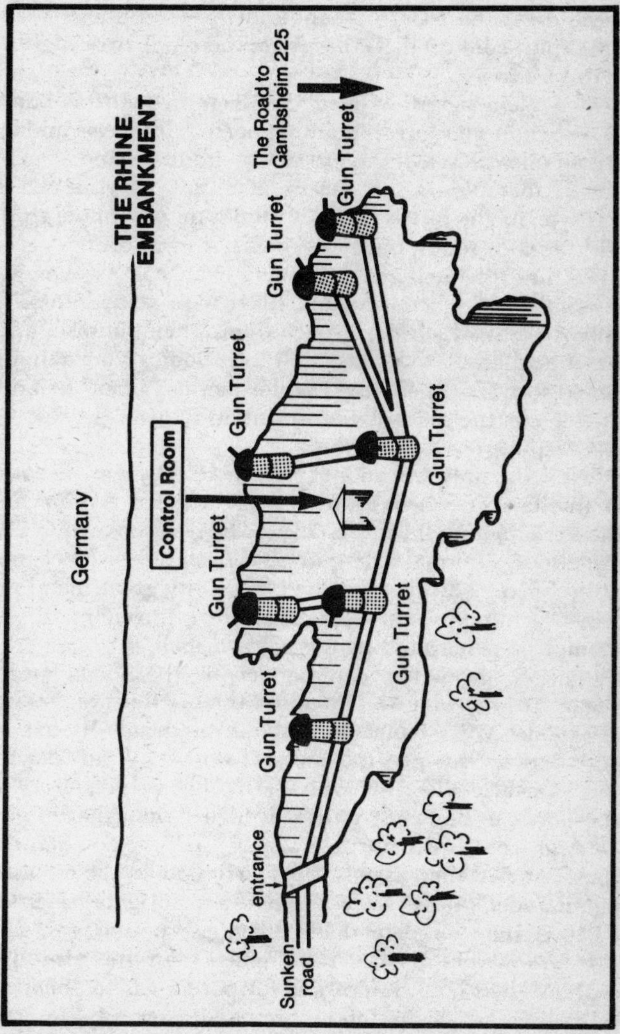

The Interior of Fort de Gambsheim

could now see of the innards of the fort. Creeping Jesus, standing by the door, bit his bottom lip. The butcher's bill for the capture of Fort de Gambsheim was going to be high, very high indeed.

Von Heinersdorff tapped the diagram with his pointer. 'These eight gun turrets pointing north, south, east and west, are all one can see of the fort above ground - and even they are retractable in an emergency. But as you can see, gentlemen, the fort is really a miniature city underground, with its own roads, barracks rooms, storage dumps etc. etc. According to intelligence the fort even has its own waste disposal unit - here! A tank filled with acid, sulphuric, I believe, into which the French dump their rubbish, and in wartime, bodies, too. One can't have bodies lying about in a closed fort, can one? Not good for morale, what!' he added, as if it was the most obvious thing in the world.

Creeping Jesus shuddered.

'Now the only entrance to Fort de Gambsheim, according to Intelligence is here to the rear of the place. As you can see the back door, as it were, is covered by two gun turrets. There are also several machine-gun posts fixed on the place too. In addition the entrance can be blocked by great metal doors which a hundred-ton tank can't break through and which cannot be penetrated by any known shell.'

'Poison gas?' the commander of the First Battalion suggested, knowing the direction the briefing was taking.

Colonel von Heinersdorff shook his head. 'It has been considered. But it, too, won't work. By an ingenious mechanical device, the whole atmospheric pressure within the Fort can be raised until it is higher than that of air.'

'And what is the purpose of that, sir?' the commander of the First Battalion asked, a little irritated by the regimental commander's slowness in answering his original question.

'It is the complete defence against poison gas. If the pressure within the Fort is higher than the atmosphere without, it is quite impossible for poison gas to penetrate.'

'Ingenious,' the battalion commander agreed. 'But is there not another entrance to the damned place?'

'As far as we know, the back door is the only entrance,' von Heinersdorff answered, swinging his silly broken sword, a look of benign happiness on his old face, as if he were very pleased with himself, though for the life of him von Schorr couldn't see why. 'Now even if an attacker does penetrate the back door, his task of conquest has only just begun. Each section of the fort is cut off from the next by an armoured steel partition, slotted for machine-gun fire, and the invader would have to attack from room to room – here, here and here – until he reached the control room – *here*!

He paused and let them follow the would-be invader's route through the underground fortress until he reached the exact centre of the place.

'The control room is naturally the nerve centre of Fort de Gambsheim. Apparently there is an enormous switchboard in the place, from which an operator can relay the commandant's orders to any part of the fort in an instant, even if they are physically cut off by an invader, and it is located fifty to sixty metres below the ground. A really difficult nut to crack,' Colonel von Heinersdorff paused for a moment, 'and it is that particular nut which the Fourth Grenadier Regiment has been ordered to crack, cost what it may.'

A wave of electric excitement ran through the room, as the officers peered at the diagram and realized just how terribly hard it was going to be. Von Heinersdorff let them have the time, sensing the young officers' excitement and telling himself that with eager young men such as these, he might well make it. For, fool that he was, even von Heinersdorff realized that the mission division had handed him was virtually suicidal.

'You see, gentlemen,' he said after a few moments, 'there has been a change in the original mission. Back in the winter it had been planned for us to merely make a feign against the Maginot Line in order to pin French troops down there, while the bulk of our forces sweep in through Belgium to the rear of the Line. Now the greater mass of the *Wehrmacht* will still attack through Belgium. But at the same time, High Command wants us to gain a limited foothold in the Line, as a bridgehead for an attack on the place itself. So how are we going to do it?' He turned to the map again. 'An assault crossing of the Rhine along the length of one kilometre, after a preliminary bombardment by the artillery of whatever French positions there are on the western bank. Thereafter, the first Battalion,' he nodded to the commander who had asked the questions, 'will fight its way up the Gambsheim road, occupying the attention of the troops manning the turrets covering the road.' He tapped the map again. 'In the meantime, the Second Battalion will swing to the front of the fort masking the guns there, while,' he paused significantly, 'the Third Battalion will attack the back door and break it open.' He stopped and looked directly at Major von Ostern, a tall blond officer in his early thirties who commanded the Third.

Von Ostern bowed stiffly, lean face revealing nothing though inside his head raged. His thousand-odd men had been virtually condemned to death. That approach road would channel them into a thickly packed mass, an ideal target for the machine-guns guarding the fort's entrance.

Happily von Heinersdorff continued his briefing. 'To cover the approach of the Third Battalion, I intend to employ those tanks you see outside. They will be floated across with the first wave, as will the bridging tanks. With a bit of luck they will head the infantry attack. Once the back door has been successfully forced, the First and Second Battalions will be whistled up to continue the attack within the fort itself. Their objective will be the place's control room, *exclusively*! Lop off the brain and the body will die of its own accord, what?' He beamed at them.

Sourly von Schorr told himself that the Old Man was really ripe for the rubber van and the funny farm. He simply had no idea of reality. In the Old War, it had taken whole divisions, even corps, to capture forts like Fort de Gambsheim at places such as Verdun. The 3000-strong Fourth Grenadiers hadn't a hope in hell of achieving their objectives.

'Well, gentlemen,' von Heinersdorff concluded. 'I must not keep you any longer. You'll want to hurry away, no doubt, and commence working out your deployment. There are only two more things I have to say to you. One is that the operation commences at dawn on the morning of May 10th. The other is,' he raised his broken sword, as if in warning, 'you must not breathe a word of this to the men. Rumours are rife as it is. On the pain of death for the individual concerned, nothing must be leaked. There must be absolute, total secrecy . . .'

'*It's off the secret list at last, sir!*' King Bull announced proudly. He extended his big hand and indicated the two strange appliances, to which Corporal Tietze was giving a last dusting with a snowy white handkerchief.

Creeping Jesus frowned, while the assembled cooks, dressed in gleaming white for the occasion, smiled fawningly at King Bull.

'But what is it?' Creeping Jesus asked, staring at the larger of two appliances, which seemed to be a metal tub on wheels, a long tin chimney sticking out of its side from which poured black smoke, and drawn by four somewhat sulky-looking horses.

'A goulash cannon, sir,' King Bull answered, his chest swelling with pride.

'A what?'

'A goulash cannon! That's what they called then in the Old War, sir, like the one you can see on the right. I had it brought from the regimental museum and adapted it personally, sir, in total secrecy.'

'So that was what the fat prick was up to all the time, Karl,' Ami whispered as the three Rebels stood at the back of the cooks. 'But what the frig is it?'

Karl shrugged. 'Search me, Ami. But no doubt he'll enlighten us in a half a mo.'

King Bull obliged. 'Sir, in the last war, the Imperial Army marched right across Western Europe, without being hungry or without a hot meal for one single day. And how was it done?' He slapped the machine from the regimental museum. 'It was done by means of this little machine.'

'But what in three devils' name is it?' Creeping Jesus cried. King Bull knew when not to press his luck too far and he was desperately anxious to please the Adjutant, especially now when action was imminent, so he said, 'It is a mobile field kitchen sir.' He turned to a fawning Corporal Tietze. 'Demonstrate, Corporal,' he barked.

'At once, sir! Immediately, sir!' Tietze replied and sprang into action. He bent and removed the spotless white cloths from the pails standing next to the larger of the two appliances to reveal diced slices of meat.

'Beef and pork, sir,' King Bull commented, 'prepared the night before, again on the march. 'One . . . two . . . three pails . . . for every two hundred and fifty litres of water,' he called, as Tietze threw the meat into the interior of the tub. 'Now, one sack of potatoes, plus carrots, and a pail of onions,' he continued as Tietze heaved ever more stuff into the tub, sweating heavily now in the heat from the fire below the tub. 'Now add salt and pepper to taste and stir. Get them nags moving, Tietze!' he barked, as the corporal took up a wooden paddle and began stirring.

'Yessir . . . At once, sir!' With the back of his boot, stirring all the while, Tietze kicked the nearest tired old horse and the team began to amble forward across the courtyard.

Slowly, as Tietze stirred as if his very life depended upon it and the three Rebels stared at the strange sight in awe, the spectators' nostrils were assailed by the first faint smell of cooking food . . .

'Goulash soup!' King Bull made a great show of the tasting the contents of the ladle, his little finger crooked at an angle to his big paw, as if he were tasting the product of some famous cook. 'Exquisite. The perfect goulash.' He gave his judgement, as the fawning cooks burst into applause.

King Bull bowed and Creeping Jesus looked interested. 'So you reckon, Bulle,' the latter said, 'that with the addition of 250 grammes of bread, one bowl of your goulash soup will keep a soldier fighting and marching for twenty-four hours?'

'I think that is correct, sir, at least my researches point in that direction,' King Bull answered, looking exceedingly modest, even seeming to blush a little.

Karl shook his head in mock wonder, as Creeping Jesus considered King Bull's invention. 'Will yer cast yer glassy orbs on the big fake,' he declared. 'All the big bastard is after is to keep himself back in the rear and let some other poor bugger risk his neck. King Bull's out to save his precious hide . . .' He spat on the ground in disgust.

'*Jawohl, Herr Hauptmann*,' King Bull was saying, 'my invention will help to win the war. Three men is all it needs – a driver, a cook and a general help. They will move up with our brave grenadiers ensuring that they receive a nourishing meal once a day, sharing the common danger, every shot and shell – and they will all be picked men, trained infantrymen who have already been under fire, ready to take up a rifle and fight at the side of the grenadiers if necessary. If I may so, sir, they – those brave men of mine – will be the Fourth Regiment's *goulash-cannon heroes*!'

'*Bravo, Oberfeld*!' Creeping Jesus said with sudden enthusiasm. 'Well said, man. The goulash-cannon heroes.' The Adjutant savoured the name, as if it were of some significance, rolling it around his tongue again. Then he said, 'Now Bulle, and who are these veteran infantrymen going to be who will man your new invention, eh?'

For a moment King Bull did not answer, but even as he opened his mouth to reply, Karl had a sudden sinking feeling. *He* knew who they were going to be. Next to him, Polack said sombrely, '*Karl, I think the big prick has gone and dropped us in the shit agen . . .*'

BOOK THREE

The Goulash Cannon Heroes

'In the time of the setting sun, dwarfs cast shadows like giants.'
Karl Kraus

CHAPTER 1

NOW IT was just before dawn on May 10th, 1940.

For five hundred miles, the whole length of the Reich's frontier with France, Luxembourg, Belgium and Holland, hundreds of thousands of young men waited for the signal to attack westwards. Down on the Rhine that single regiment, the Fourth Grenadiers, which would be the first to invade France, the heriditary enemy since 1914, waited too.

Tense and expectant, their nerves tingling electrically, each man wrapped in a cocoon of his own thoughts, the young grenadiers crouched in their jump-off positions, staring as if mesmerized at the lazy silver snake of the Rhine and the dark mysterious smudge, which was France, beyond. Now their officers, eyes fixed on the green-glowing dials of their watches, began to count off the seconds.

Once again Karl patted the nervous horse. It shied and trembled as did the others pulling the goulash cannon, as if the beasts already knew what lay in store for them on the other side of the Rhine; as if the nervousness of the young soldiers crouched in the field all around them had communicated itself to them. Polack urinated for the umpteenth time, cursing softly to himself in Polish because of his jumpiness. Ami sucked on an unlit cigarette as a baby might do on its mother's breast for comfort. Even Karl was somehow comforted by the animal warmth of the nervous horses.

Karl Carstens was not a fanciful man, but at that moment before it all started he could visualize the thousands of other young men like himself waiting to undergo the lethal violence to come, wondering what it would be like and whether they would survive this May 10th, which would change the history of the world. He cast a look around at the anxious white blurs of faces about him. They were the assault wave. How many of them would be dead within the hour? How many?

'*Ten seconds*!' an officer hissed.

'*Ten seconds, lads . . . ten seconds, do you hear?*' the NCOs called softly. '*Ten seconds . . . ten seconds . . .*' the words went down the line. The nearest horse whinnied softly, as if in protest.

Next to Karl, Polack began to count off the seconds to himself in Polish. Ami gulped and threw away his cigarette, angrily, as if he felt fate was being unjust to him for having brought him to this place this dawn.

Over the French positions a single flare sailed effortlessly into the sky, hung there in an eerie unreal green light for a moment before sinking to the ground like a fallen angel.

'*Zero!*' Polack hissed.

As if some invisible hand had thrown a giant power switch, a tremendous flash of scarlet flame split the dawn greyness. For one long electric second, the air tingled and trembled. Awe-struck, the attackers stared at the sky, their hearts thumping like crazy trip-hammers. With startling suddenness, the whole horizon erupted in violent flame, as the German barrage descended upon France. Heavy railway guns thundered. Field artillery belched fire. Mortars howled. Four hundred shells struck home, as the god of war drew his first terrifying breath. Suddenly the very earth beneath them began to quiver and tremble like a live thing. Men screamed. Others gulped for air, as if they were choking. A few even put their hands over their eyes like frightened children attempting to blot out some horrific nightmare.

But this nightmare would not go away.

Abruptly officers were springing out of their hiding places everywhere, waving their pistols. NCOs yelled orders. Others shrilled on their whistles. '*Hurrah . . . hurrah!*' the grenadiers cried with sudden crazy enthusiasm, as they started to push their assault boats out of the bushes. Grimly, face suddenly lathered in sweat in spite of the coolness of the morning, Karl held onto the horses, which plunged and tore in fright, as to their front the horizon started to disappear in thick black smoke, tinged here and there by bright cherry-red flame.

Now the smaller German guns were concentrating on the bank opposite. Phosphorus shells streamed flatly across the river, trailing furious white sparks behind them. They exploded in bursts of cream-coloured flame. Tracer zipped towards the enemy positions. Here and there a *poilu** panicked, burst out of his hole, ran screaming from it, a living torch that abruptly tottered, spun round, attempted to beat out the greedy all-consuming flames with hands that were themselves already ablaze.

Now the men were in their boats. '*Los*!' the officers cried. The men began to paddle furiously, as if their lives depended upon it. Watching, eyes filled with awed horror, Karl prayed that they would make it safely to the other bank. Surely nothing could live in that hellish inferno?

But Karl was wrong. A single flare sailed into the burning sky from the French side. It must have been a signal. Almost immediately, a line of fire ran the length of the French bank, machine-gun bullets hissing towards the men in the little boats in their thousands. The first wave simply disappeared. In an instant, the sinking, bullet-riddled boats were drifting helplessly, filled with a cargo of dead and dying grenadiers. Scores of men were struggling in the boiling water, floundering and screaming, being dragged down by the weight of their equipment. 'Oh my God,' Karl moaned impotently, 'they're being massacred out there!'

But already the next wave was pushing off from the bank, urged on by angry NCOs, aiming kicks at their backsides when they were too slow for this date with death. Again the wall of French fire struck them. Karl wished he could close his eyes and blot out the slaughter. But he couldn't. He had to watch.

But now as the third wave began to push itself through what remained of the first two, paddling ruthlessly through the wounded, struggling and yelling piteously for help in the water, the first of the attackers began to reach the opposite bank. Slugs scythed the length of the shallow water. A whole group of field-greys went down in a crazy huddle, spitting and gurgling, drowning where they lay. But there were ever

*'Hairy': nickname for a French private soldier

more, splashing crazily forward through the carpet of bodies only to run straight into the mines and wire.

The fourth wave came in, urged by their officers, shrilling their whistles, screaming exhortations, waving their pistols. They rushed the minefield, littered with the shattered bodies of their comrades, and hit the wire. There they, too, were mown down in their turn. Unable to advance or withdraw, they stopped there, some of them trapped by the barbs almost like dumb animals waiting for the inevitable slaughter.

Now the tanks started to waddle forward, while Karl and his comrades watched the slaughter in open-mouthed horror. Like ducks they entered the water. A flurry of bubbles, the enemy bullets whipping up spray all around them, and they disappeared, the only sign that they had not sunk for good the smoke coming from an exhaust which had been placed above their turrets.

Now more and more soaked grenadiers were reaching the opposite bank, baulking at the barbed wire fences, some of them hanging there like so many bloodstained scarecrows, twitching weakly each time another bullet slammed into their torn flesh. But even that obstacle was being overcome by sheer weight of numbers, as the attackers advanced as if against pelting rain, bodies bent and tensed for the impact of that first slug.

Suddenly, startlingly, the first Mark III burst from the Rhine near the opposite bank. Shaking water from it like a wet dog, it rolled over the dead, crunching their bodies to a blood-red pulp under its flailing tracks, and started to ascend the bank, splattering blood and mud behind it. Hurriedly grenadiers formed up behind it, grateful for its metal-skinned protection. The Mark III waddled on, its stubby cannon spitting fire. Tracer howled off its side like glowing ping-pong balls. But nothing could stop the metal monster. Like a primeval monster seeking out its prey, its turret swung from left to right, knocking out the French positions one by one.

French infantry took up the challenge. They came running out of the wood to the right, crying '*A l'attaque*!' and '*Vive la France*!'

'*Sieg Heil . . . Sieg Heil!*' came the answering cry from a hundred young throats, as the two lines clashed. Teeth shone in blackened oily faces. Eyes like those of madmen gleamed dementedly. Obscene animal sounds came from their throats. Locked together in hand-to-hand combat, they slashed, gouged, hacked, chopped, sliced, tore, ripped at each other. Rifles were useless now. They were replaced by bayonets, knives, shovels, knives, boots, bare hands, as the battle for the west bank of the Rhine entered its first crucial phase.

'*Third Battalion will embark now!*' Major von Ostern's voice was clear above the noise of the grim battle being waged on the other side of the Rhine. '*Into the boats!*'

Dawn had come reluctantly, as if hesitant to illuminate that terrible lunar landscape below. Now as the three Rebels urged the nags pulling the goulash cannon onto the raft on which they would cross, they could see the mess of war littering the opposite bank. A wrecked Mark III, the bloody sweep of mud, the corpses everywhere, the mushrooms of black smoke rising to the ugly grey sky. All was violent death and horror.

Now the engineers started to paddle energetically, while the Rebels hung onto the quivering terrified horses, which started violently at every fresh detonation. Tracer started to float their way, lazily at first, then gathering speed at a tremendous rate so that it seemed they were heading straight for a glowing wall of white fire. Men of the Third started to scream with pain. Arms flailing the air wildly, they went over the side. At Karl's feet one of the paddlers stopped suddenly and just sat there, head hanging down as if he'd just nodded off.

'Get that frigging paddle working!' the sergeant in charge snapped angrily. 'Move yersen!'

'I can't, Sarge,' the paddler answered miserably. He held up his left arm. His hand was hanging from the gory mess of his bullet-shattered wrist by a few shreds of flesh. Karl looked away hastily, throat filling with sour bile.

A tremendous howl. A French Moraine fighter fell out of the leaden sky, machine-guns chattering. Not for long. A lucky shell caught it in mid-dive. It burst apart in the air, its severed wings fluttering down like metallic leaves.

A crippled motor launch zig-zagged madly through the field-grey corpses bobbing up and down in their lifebelts, its racing propellors churning the bodies into a red pulp. A screaming soldier with no hands trying to swim. A lone survivor in a boat filled with dead, kneeling and praying, oblivious to the murder and mayhem all around him. A sergeant, his shattered face streaming down on to his chest like molten red wax. . . And all set against this terrible backdrop of flames, smoke and sudden, violent death.

Karl's raft was half way across when it happened. There was a great clanging boom. The horses reared up in terror. A sheet of bright red flame rent the smoke. The raft heaved and dipped. There was the crack of breaking timbers. Suddenly they were up to their ankles in water, ears assailed by curses, cries, pleas for help, someone crying desperately for his mother, and then they were sinking rapidly . . .

CHAPTER 2

PAPA PONTIVY took his time. Calmly he rolled a cigarette with his one hand, pressing it together against his bemedalled chest, before putting it in his mouth and accepting a light from Captain Mercier, whose anxiety was all too obvious. Papa took a few drags, the spittle from his mouth already soaking through the thin paper. As always Papa Pontivy, commandant of Fort de Gambsheim was not a pretty smoker. Mercier waited for him to speak, the sound of gunfire muted by the thick concrete walls about them.

A miniature train clattered by them, laden with more shells for the gun turrets and a handful of 'shellfish', as Papa called them, their khaki berets adorned with the badge of the fortress troops – a concrete casemate upon a field of barbed wire.

Papa rolled his cigarette to the corner of his mouth, old eyes suddenly very red. '*Bon*, Mercier, this is what I think will happen.'

His second-in-command was instantly alert. The commandant was a veteran of this sort of thing. Had he not lost his left hand at Fort Vaux in Verdun in the Old War? This was not the first time he had undergone an attack of this kind.

'They will succeed in crossing the Rhine. Our outposts are already pulling back, and before division readies a force for an effective counter-attack,' he shrugged and spat on the concrete floor in disgust (Papa Pontivy had never thought much of headquarters), '*eh bien*, for a while we will be on our own. So what will the Boche attempt to do?' He tugged Mercier's arm and they began to walk through the yellow gloom of the fort towards the lift. 'They will mask us and then attack us from the rear – the backdoor. That's the way they did it at Vaux and at Douamont* and that is the way they'll

*Another of the fortresses of Verdun.

do it this time as well. The Boche never learn very rapidly.' He chuckled and pressed his cigarette which threatened to fall apart at any moment.

They entered the lift, which like the observation turret to which it led was made of reinforced steel, capable of stopping any known German shell. Mercier pressed the button. Noiselessly they began to ascend to the surface. Papa puffed stolidly at his cigarette. To Mercier, he looked like a man who did not have a care in the world, despite the fact that his command was imminently threatened by a full-scale enemy attack.

The lift stopped and they stepped into the observation turret, manned by two of the 'shellfish'. They clicked to attention and Papa waved for them to stand at ease. He stepped to the slit and peered out for a few moments, while Mercier did the same at the other slit.

To their front, the landscape had been transformed since they had last seen it. Now everywhere there were shell-holes, brown and steaming like the work of gigantic moles. Through gaps in the smoke of war, they could catch glimpses of running figures, some in field-grey, some in the khaki of the French Army. But that was about all. If there *was* a whole regiment of Boche out there, Papa Pontivy told himself, there were few signs of them. Had their attack bogged down already? He rose from the slit with a sigh.

Next to him Mercier did the same, putting his own thoughts into words. 'If we only knew what was going on out there, sir!' He exclaimed. 'Those damn telephone lines!'

'It is always the same,' Papa said calmly and spat out his cigarette. 'The lines are usually the first to go out. But no matter. Let us understand that we must rely on ourselves for the time being.' He nodded to the two shellfish. 'Just keep a sharp look-out, boys,' he said, 'and let me know the instant you spot anything moving in front of the fort towards the rear, understood?'

'*Bien entendu, mon Commandant*!' the taller of the two replied smartly in the heavily accented French of an Alsatian native.

Papa frowned. Yet another of those wretched Alsatians in

his garrison. Wordlessly he took Mercier by the arm and they re-entered the lift, bound for his command post. It was only when they were moving again that he expressed his doubts to his young second-in-command. 'Whatever the Boche do, we can hold for days, even weeks if necessary, if the men's nerves hold.' He began to roll himself another cigarette against his chest.

'You mean the local reserves, sir?'

'Yes. I have taken the greatest care in the selection of my garrison here, but I cannot guarantee every man in it. This mixed population here in Alsace means that the local reserves are not as loyal as they should be. Nazi propaganda has appealed to their nationalism, and besides,' he stuck the loosely rolled cigarette into the corner of his mouth, 'why should they fire on men who could well be of the same blood as themselves, even related?'

Mercier tended him a light again and nodded his agreement. 'They're a strange lot, indeed, sir. Only last week I came across some of their children, who had nailed an owl to the church door and were poking its eyes out with pointed sticks. They said owls drink oil from the church lamps and go and chuckle in some hole in the belfry when the death knell is tolled. That's why they were torturing the poor creature.' He shuddered at the memory of the owl, nailed by its wings to the old oaken church-door, the blood streaming down from the scarlet hole where the laughing, barefoot peasant children had poked out its eye.

'Inbreeding, you know, Mercier,' Papa said, as they entered the busy command post, the typewriters clattering, the telephonists issuing a stream of orders to the various perimeter positions. 'They've had five hundred years of breeding with their own kind, and my brave French shellfish have not had much opportunity, cooped up down here, to inject much new blood into their women.' He chuckled and Mercier reminded himself that Papa Pontivy still spent most of his leaves in the brothels of Metz and Nancy, in spite of his sixty-odd years.

'So,' Papa was serious again, 'our only real problem is the

loyalty of those local reserves. As long as the Boche are outside the fort, they'll remain true to France. But if the Boche succeed in forcing the backdoor . . .' he shrugged expressively.

'I shall ensure that the men manning the machine-guns covering the entrance are all Frenchmen from the interior, sir,' Mercier said hurriedly.

'Excellent idea –'

'Sir!'

Papa swung round. One of the operators was waving his arm excitedly, scribbling furiously on his pad all the while with the other. With surprising speed for such an old man, Papa strode across the big room towards him. 'What is it, Corporal?' he demanded, instinctively knowing that the trouble had commenced.

'The Germans have broken through the Rhine line, sir . . . One of the observation posts is taking a flag signal from the infantry . . . They are falling back, sir . . .' Without taking his eyes off his pad, the operator gasped out the information, face flushed and excited. 'Enemy pressure too intense . . . They report they will seek shelter in the fort if permission is granted . . . Over and out.'

'Permission granted!' Papa barked immediately. 'The more men we have inside Fort de Gambsheim, the happier I will be. Get on with it, Corporal.'

'Sir!' The operator began to talk rapidly into the phone, the sweat glistening on his forehead like opaque pearls.

Papa turned away and glanced at his watch. 'So, Mercier, it looks as if we can expect *Messieurs les Boches* in about an hour.'

'So long?'

Papa nodded. 'You are forgetting our little obstacle, Mercier. They will get through it, of course, in the end. But it will come as a nasty surprise and will dampen their ardour, no doubt.' He chuckled softly but there was no warmth in the laugh.

Now it was Mercier's turn to frown. 'It is against the international rules of land warfare, sir,' he protested, as he had protested when Papa had ordered the removing of the warning signs back in December after the unsuccessful German raid.

Papa moved his damp cigarette to the corner of his old mouth, where it clung as if glued to his bottom lip. 'My dear Mercier,' he rasped harshly, 'when it comes to the defence of France, old Papa knows no rules of land warfare. This is the second time the Boche have invaded our beloved country in my life-time. Let them pay the price, however horrible. Now on your way, Mercier. Alert the gate to expect the retreating infantry - and Mercier.'

'Sir?' The young officer paused, noting the iron resolution in the old man's pale face beneath the mop of snow-white hair that had gained him his nickname.

'Don't forget those machine-gunners.'

'No sir, I won't.'

'Ensure too that one of them is sited with his machine-gun pointing *into* the fort - just in case.' Mercier gasped with surprise and said, 'You mean, sir -'

'I mean nothing, Mercier!' Papa cut him short and spitting out his damp cigarette end commenced rolling yet another with his one hand . . .

Five minutes later Captain Mercier had issued his orders and the swarthy, undersized machine-gunners from Provence hurried to set up their Hotchkiss next to the great steel door, its muzzle pointing straight down the road which led into the fort's interior. Thereafter Mercier hurried back to the command post where Papa awaited him, trying to avoid the look of hate in the eyes of those 'shellfish' who came from Alsace. For they knew now what Papa intended. At the first sign of surrender or mutiny, the one-armed commandant of Fort de Gambsheim would mow them down without mercy . . .

CHAPTER 3

FROM ALL sides came cries, shouts, yells of agony. Boats were sinking or in flames everywhere. As the three Rebels lashed their terrified horses, forcing them up the muddy, body-littered embankment, another assault boat down below went up in flames as it was hit. Madly the trapped soldiers tried to beat out the flames that engulfed them. In vain, they tore at their white flesh, turning into a black bubbling pulp, from which the blood oozed scarlet like the juice of an overripe fig.

With one last desperate heave the three of them shoved the goulash cannon over the top of the embankment, forced the horses to their knees and collapsed, the choking black smoke from the burning boat mercifully hiding them for a while from the enemy gunners.

There were bodies everywhere, exposed with all their terrible mutilations: the bloody stumps where arms had been blown off; smashed-in ribs, revealing the dirty-white pulp of shattered lungs, ripped-open guts, the obscene grey contents strewn on the grass like ghastly white squashed slugs. '*Boshe moi*!' Polack whispered, appalled, and crossed himself hastily. 'It looks as if somebody worked them over with a blunt can-opener!'

'Come on, you cooks,' a hearty voice broke into their horror-stricken reverie. 'Everyone's needed up front. Get that goulash cannon, or whatever you call it moving. *Los!*'

Hurriedly they rose to their feet, and snapped to attention. It was Colonel von Heinersdorff, still carrying his silly broken-off sword, though this time he had a pistol in his other hand. He beamed at them inanely, as if this was all very good fun, the dead grenadiers all around seemingly unnoticed. 'What battalion are you with, Grenadiers?'

'With the Third, sir,' Karl replied.

'Oh, they're over there somewhere. Off you go!' He waved his sword vaguely towards the right and then disappeared into the smoke as abruptly as he had appeared. Karl looked at the others, then he shrugged. 'No use trying to dodge it, comrades. Some bugger like Creeping Jesus'll be prowling around as well, and we don't want to get reported. Cos you know what that would mean.' He clicked his forefinger, as if pulling a trigger.

Ami shivered. 'Yer, you're right, Karl,' he agreed. 'Old Creeping Jesus'd have us in front of a firing squad for cowardice in the face of the enemy in zero comma nothing seconds. Let's go.'

Polack cracked his whip and the four old nags started to move once more, towing the cart behind them, their flanks twitching nervously, nostrils distended with fear, as they sensed instinctively that they were in mortal danger.

Now they passed the dead of the waves that had gone before them, their tunics ripped open to reveal torn and gashed flesh, pulpy and a glistening red like fresh meat in a butcher's window. Their bodies were sack-like, yet stiff. Fists were clenched as if in anger at their fate. Genitals protruded from burst-open flies like wax fruit. Eyes were not quite shut, but leered, or so it seemed, with a grizzly sheen. Lips were drawn back, teeth bared in a last animal snarl. Some were minus heads; others minus legs and arms – featureless packages of gory red meat. And there were dozens of them, row after row, slaughtered in formation. The whole place stank of violent death.

Sickened by the carnage, trying to hold onto the horses, which twitched and jittered at the sight of so much death, the three Rebels advanced grimly along this dreadful route through the charnel house, the sound of the firing getting louder and telling them they would soon be reaching the scene of the action . . .

Crump . . . crump . . . Crump!

A tremendous salvo of French shells rocked their front. Bushes and trees were lashed almost level with the ground, as the hot wind of blast struck them across the face like a blow from a flabby fist. The lead horse reared up on its hindlegs, tugging, crazy with fear, at the traces. Polack, exerting all his strength, just managed to hold the terrified beast as a dead cow slammed into the field ahead and somehow or other disintegrated. Why, the scared Rebels did not know or care at that particular moment; for each fresh detonation was stupefying, pulverizing, horrific. They concentrated solely on remaining alive, as they stumbled on through the bombardment across that pitted, smoking, lunar landscape.

'Over there – that barn!' Karl yelled above the banshee-like howl of more shells. 'We'll take cover there!'

Polack lashed the horses cruelly across their gleaming flanks and they clattered on, the goulash cannon bouncing up and down on the rough ground, the rusty wire which had once borne those grim warning signs unnoticed, as yet once again the field to their right exploded for no apparent reason.

It was the dying officer who alerted them to their terrible danger. They had almost reached the barn, all the time followed by the French shells, as if the unseen enemy gunners were pursuing a personal feud with them, when he crawled into view, his left leg vanished at the hip, his face looking as if someone had just thrown a handful of strawberry jam at it. 'Stop there!' he cried weakly, sitting and waving his hands. 'Stop there!'

'But they're shelling us, sir!' Karl called back a little helplessly, as fist-sized pieces of red-hot shrapnel cut the air all around them alarmingly.

'Stop there!' the dying officer repeated weakly, his life-force ebbing from him visibly, as he shook his head like a boxer refusing to go down for a count of ten.

'But it's dangerous here, sir!' Karl answered, as Polack fought the terrified horses, which were plunging and rearing, threatening to break the traces at any moment. 'We'll be killed!'

The officer waved his hand once more and called something, which was drowned by yet another salvo of shells plunging out of the burning sky. Then he said, just before he pitched forward on his face, dead, one single word which made their blood curdle, '*Mines* . . !'

'For God's sake, be careful, Karl,' Ami whispered tensely, as Karl began to crawl, bayonet clenched in a hand wet with sweat. Behind him Polack had forced the horses onto their knees, having blindfolded them to blot out the terrible scene. Still they trembled violently and Polack, holding the reins, was crimson-faced with the effort of trying to hold them.

Karl put his hands down in front of him carefully. Nothing happened! Gingerly, very gingerly, he swept his hand around to left and right, feeling for the deadly little prong which would indicate the mine below. Again nothing. He sighed with relief and kept on with his terribly slow progress as the shells continued to rain down.

Sweating like a frightened pig, hardly daring to breathe, each fresh advance made only after what seemed an age of deliberation, Karl advanced at a snail's pace, testing out the soft ground bit by bit. He knew the urgency of his mission – the other two cowering to his rear could be hit at any moment – but there was no other way to do it. On and on he went, the minutes ticking by leadenly.

Suddenly, startlingly, he felt it. His heart almost stopped beating. But there was no denying it. A small forked metal prong. *A mine!*

For a moment he was paralysed, unable to move. But only for a moment. He couldn't risk the others' lives a minute more than necessary. With his bayonet, he cleared the earth around the deadly little device and then, dropping the weapon, began to feel gingerly underneath it. No matchbox fuse.* No trip-wire connecting it with another mine so that if it was lifted carelessly it would set off the other one.

Hastily he took out the fuse and lifted it with hands that were suddenly trembling like leaves. Now he was coming ever

*A spring-loaded fuse shaped like a metal matchbox. Once the pressure is released, the spring activates the fuse and explodes under the mine.

closer to a ditch bordering on a farmtrack and he told himself that that would be the edge of the minefield. Once they reached the ditch, they would be safe – for a while anyway. He knelt there and cried, 'All right, Polack start leading the horses. Keep them between the two tracks I've scored with my bayonet. And for Chrissake, hold a tight rein on 'em!'

Polack was too nervous to answer; he didn't trust his own voice. So he just nodded and, holding the rein with a big hand that was an ivory-white at the knuckles with strain, he clicked his tongue for the terrified blindfolded horses to advance. Behind him Ami clung to the goulash cannon, his gaze fixed hypnotically on the ground, advancing in tiny trippling little steps.

Karl crawled on. His clothes were wet with sweat. He could feel his soaked underpants clinging to his crotch unpleasantly, while his breath came in short hectic little gasps. He hit another mine. With fingers that felt like clumsy sausages, he started to check it out. Again nothing. No trip-wire, no booby-trap. He freed the ugly device from the earth and crouched there on his knees, all energy drained from him. How he longed to just lie there, let it happen. What did anything matter any more?

'Karl, we're just behind you,' Polack's anxious whisper roused him from his lethargy.

'Right, moving on,' he forced himself to say in a shaky uncertain voice, which he hardly recognized as his own.

And then it happened. From the rear came the sounds of orders in German and a harsh voice yelling, '*Los . . . los . . . dalli . . . dalli*! Move those lead arses of yourn! The frogs have got this shitting field bracketed . . .'

Face contorted with horror, Karl twisted his head. In a gap in the smoke, he could see field-grey infantry crowding together as the edge of the field, while a tall figure, perhaps an officer, urged them to move forward.

He cupped his hands to his mouth. '*Stop*!' he began to scream. But it was already too late. The men were running straight into the minefield, urged on by the over-eager officer, who was running with them, waving his pistol as if it were a sword and this was some brave 19th century charge as depicted in a romantic battle-painting of the time.

What happened next was in no way romantic. The first mine exploded, scattering bodies everywhere, arms and legs flailing wildly in the same instant that the second one went off – and the third. Suddenly mines were exploding under their running feet everywhere and in an instant the field was turned into a slaughter-house, and the charge was stopped dead. Papa Pontivy's cruel little trick of removing the warning notices around the minefield had worked and for the time being the attack of the Fourth Grenadiers had been stopped.

Sadly trying to shut out the plaintive cries of the wounded, Karl continued his task, as the battlefield fell strangely silent, almost as if the French who had sprung this murderous trick on the attackers were ashamed of what they had done and were sick of the slaughter.

Ten minutes later he was through to the ditch. Karl flung one look back at that body-littered, shattered field, saw the man on his knees staring at his stumps, as if he could not believe that this was happening to *him*, and turned sickened. Wordlessly, even the old horses silent and subdued now, they began to plod towards the ruined barn. Above them the bright blue of the morning had given way to a leaden sky, ominous and threatening. There was going to be a storm.

CHAPTER 4

THE SICKLE moon cast a cold spectral light on the shell-shattered trees. An owl hooted far off. Otherwise all was silent, tense expectation. Now the rain had stopped and the track glistened in the moonlight, as they stole forward to the attack.

While the storm had raged, Major von Ostern had collected together the remnants of the shattered companies, some from his own battalion, others from the remaining two grenadier battalions. As the shocked survivors had filed into the ruined barn to be fed from the Rebels' bubbling goulash cannon he had declared with more confidence than he felt, 'Comrades, they think they have beaten us. They will never expect us to attack this night. But we will and we'll surprise – *and beat 'em*!' Over and over he had repeated the same message, while the grenadiers gobbled down the meagre fare to make room for the others waiting outside in the bitter rain. In the end even Karl had almost half believed the tall blond young officer.

Up on the hill, which concealed the underground fort, yet another flare hissed into the silver night. The column stopped at once. The Rebels tensed, clapping their hands over the muzzles of the horses to prevent them making any noise. The flare exploded. Instantly everything was bathed in the eerie red light. Nothing moved. Slowly it fell, to expire in the wet grass like a hissing, writhing snake. Again a heavy brooding silence descended upon the column. But there was no firing. Once more they had not been spotted.

Major von Ostern, standing at the side of the track, armed solely with a stick, nodded to the Rebels. 'Roof-hare for lunch, I suppose, cooks*?' he quipped in a hushed whisper.

Even Polack managed a smile, as Ami snapped back,

*Soldiers' name for cat.

'Roof-hare it is, sir, plus half a litre of fart soup per man, *per-haps*.'

Von Ostern shook his stick at them in mock anger. 'Get along with you, you disrespectful lot. Fart soup, indeed!'

They plodded on, every eye fixed on the dark smudge of the hill, waiting for that first electric burst of fire which would indicate that they had been spotted.

'I would say, Mercier,' Papa Pontivy said slowly, rolling his wet cigarette from one side of his mouth to the other, 'that the only thing that makes life worth living for your private soldier is cunt.' He said the word without emphasis. All the same Mercier blushed a little at the crudity of it. He rubbed his unshaven chin to hide his embarrassment and said, 'What about their country, their sense of duty, patriotism, sir?'

'Claptrap for politicians and high ranking generals, Mercier,' Papa said cynically and without taking his cigarette from his mouth, took a drink from the mug of red wine in front of him on the command post table. 'Take away the common soldier's hope that one day soon he will be sticking his evil organ into some willing female, and his will to resist vanishes. Cunt,' again he did not emphasize the word, 'is your average soldier's only link with life itself.' He laughed wearily.

Tired as they were after the long day of battle, the unshaven operators grinned at Papa's words. The Old Man was living up to his reputation. Only the senior signaller, Walter, a local, did not share their humour; but then the Alsatians were notoriously prudish, running to the local Catholic church on the slightest pretext.

'Did you know, Mercier,' Papa continued, 'that when it was decided to make Marshal Petain commander of the Verdun battle back in '16, the officers sent to tell him of the appointment found him in a Parisian brothel – and that at the age of sixty-nine!' Papa puffed out his wrinkled cheeks expansively, wet cigarette still glued to his bottom lip. 'Now a man like that deserved to succeed in battle.' He took another sip at the coarse issue red wine. 'In essence, you can forget all your fancy tactics and all the rest of it, Mercier. This is the only lesson a battle commander need learn – the man who can't fuck, or isn't allowed to fuck, well that man won't fight!'

Mercier smiled nervously and the operators laughed, save Walter, whose gaze had now taken in the winking red light on the panel facing the operator nearest him. 'Bojax,' he commanded in that harsh accented French of his, 'there is a message on your line. Attend to it!'

'Sergeant,' Bojax answered and pulled out the plug with his left hand while he held the earphone closer to his head with the other. Hastily he began to scribble on the pad in front of him. 'Sir,' he said urgently.

Mercier rose to his feet, automatically buttoning his tunic, as if he already knew a message at this time of the night could only mean trouble. At the table Papa drained the rest of his mug in one swallow, and waited, while Mercier read through the message the operator had handed him.

'A listening post has spotted the Boche, sir!' Mercier snapped hurriedly. 'They're coming up the track to the south-west. The exact number of them is not known. But the listening post guesses they are in battalion strength.'

Papa nodded his understanding, and fastened his tunic too. 'All right, Mercier, this is it – the attack on the back door! Warn all posts. Raise the air pressure in case –' He didn't finish his sentence. He knew just how much these young soldiers of his feared poison gas. 'And alert the – er – special machine-gun team,' he added, as he started to buckle on his pistol awkwardly.

'Yessir. Will do, sir,' Mercier replied, and hurried away, to be followed a moment later by Papa himself. Walter watched his back as he went, a frown on his face. Would the dirty old man really turn the gun on his own men? he asked himself. 'Yes, he would,' a harsh little voice at the back of his mind hissed, '*especially if they happened to be Alsatians . . .*'

For most of the next hour or so, the Germans, lurking outside the fort like grey ghosts, tried to draw the fire of the *poilus* defending the sector of the place facing the Rhine. It was von Ostern's plan to engage the sector in a fire-fight as a feint, while his main force infiltrated the gate area. His grenadiers were recklessly brave in their attempts to make the French defenders open fire. More than once they exposed themselves, standing bolt upright in the moonlight, challenging the French to shoot them. At other times they sang, cursed loudly, and rattled their canteens, making a great deal of noise. Some called out in French, '*Aidez-moi, comrades . . . je suis blessé*!'

But the trick didn't work. All the French speaker got for his pains was '*Sale con.* I'll help you all right . . . With my bayonet up yer Boche arse!'

The calls in French were followed by sudden screams, moans of pain and electrifying yells, as blood-chilling as the cry of an epileptic in the throes of an attack. But none of this drew French fire. 'A war of nerves,' Papa commented, 'simply a war of nerves, Mercier.'

The young Captain nodded his agreement, looking at the Alsatians manning this sector out of the corner of his eye. They were pale and jumpy, he could see that, but they were obeying the commandant's orders to the letter. None of them had even made an attempt to fire.

Five minutes later there was the high-pitched hysterical chatter of a heavy German machine-gun. Tracer zipped towards their observation post and Mercier could hear the ricochets howling off the steel plating. 'Take that, you rotten frog pigs!' an angry voice called. '*Kameraden von Elsass, warum kämpft ihr für die Franzmänner? Ihr seid doch Deutsche!*'*

Papa spoke little German, but he caught the German word for 'Alsace' easily enough and knew instinctively that the Boche were making an appeal to his locally recruited troops. 'Machine-gunner,' he called to the nearest gunner, 'give them a burst. At once!'

The man flushed and hesitated, suddenly nervous.

*'Comrades from Alsace, why do you fight for the frogs? You are German!'

'You heard me,' Papa spat out his cigarette angrily. '*FIRE!*'

'*Oui, mon Commandant*!' the Alsatian said and pressed his trigger. Instantly the chamber was flooded with the stink of burned cordite, the noise ear-splitting.

From outside there was a howl, whether fake or genuine, the defenders did not know. But suddenly the shouts and jeers and appeals ceased. Abruptly all was as quiet as the grave and a suddenly uneasy Papa realized that the Boche were beginning to win the war of nerves. His Alsatians were definitely jumpy . . .

'Mercier,' he whispered taking his second-in-command to one side, 'watch them!' And the latter did not need to be told who Papa meant.

Cautiously, very cautiously, Major von Ostern raised his head over the concrete wall and stared down at the road below. There was no sign of the enemy. But he knew they were there, hidden in their bolt-holes that covered the entrance to Fort de Gambsheim. He sucked his teeth and told himself it was going to be a hairy one. There was only room enough on the road for a squad at a time to assault down it and they would be easy meat for the French gunners, protected by a metre or so of reinforced concrete. His only hope of getting close enough for his men to dig in and begin a co-ordinated attack on the entrance was the men crouching nervously next to him, laden down by the cumbersome pack which went with their terrible weapon.

A hundred metres away, down in the hollow, the three Rebels prepared the goulash cannon for the battle to come. Carefully they tied rags around the hooves of the nervous horses to prevent them slipping on the wet concrete. The oven came next. They extinguished the fire with wet earth, scattering the ashes carefully. Now they began to lower King Bull's patent tin chimney so that it faced the rear of the stove and gave it more headroom. 'Looks like a frigging cannon now, Karl,' Ami said, as they fastened the pipe down with wire.

'For Chrissake, don't say that,' Karl growled. 'You'll have every frigging frog gunner taking potshots at us thinking we're the real thing!'

Little did Karl know just how effective the goulash cannon's appearance was going to be in the battle to come.

Now Major von Ostern hesitated no longer. The French were alerted, that was certain. For all he knew they were already readying their reserves for a counter-attack - and in two hours' time it would be dawn. It was now or never. He swept his arm to the left. The first of the two assault companies started clambering down the bank which led to the approach road. Now to the right. The second assault company began to creep stealthily over the roof over the fort to the right of the entrance. If the door were forced, they would *drop* right into action. Now the two reserves companies, to which the Rebels belonged, started to march to the rear, waiting for their call to action.

Impatiently von Ostern counted off the minutes, calculating the time it would take his various companies to reach their jumping off points. Carefully he raised his pistol and pressed the trigger. The pistol barked, sounding like the knell of doom, followed an instant later by a nerve-racking silence. But the men whom von Ostern now lead down the slope to the road below were without nerves and without emotions. They had to be in their cruel trade. Clumsily they began to waddle down the slope towards the road, with von Ostern in the lead. The second phase of the battle for Fort de Gambsheim was about to commence . . .

CHAPTER 5

'VORWAERTS!' VON Ostern's voice shattered the heavy silence. He dropped the last three metres to the road.

In that very same moment, the machine-gun in the nearest tower spat fire. Tracer bullets hissed through the silver darkness. On the slope one of the grenadiers, guarding the men with the packs, screaming in naked, unashamed agony, bloody buttonholes stitched across his tunic, came rolling down the slope. Another flung up his arms, as if he had already abandoned all hope, and fell backwards, blood jetting from his throat in a bright scarlet arc. But the rest came on, the men with the packs panting with the effort.

Now von Ostern, as he crouched there, legs spread and slightly bent like a western gunslinger, could see the entrance to the fort quite clearly: the stout metal door, covered on both sides by concrete towers, from which machine-guns protruded.

As he began to snap off single shots at the machine-gun apertures, seemingly oblivious to the bullets cutting the air all around him, the tall young Major reasoned that they just might force that door, if their effort was concentrated enough. The first of the men with the packs lumbered up, accompanied by his bodyguard, panting heavily. 'My orders, sir?' he gasped.

'Tower at the left *Quick!* Aim for the machine-gun aperture.' Von Ostern emptied his magazine at the tower as he saw the deadly machine-gun swing round in the direction of the new arrivals. The man with the pack needed no urging. He knew just how dangerously vulnerable he was. He thrust up his hose. There was a deep sigh like some primeval monster drawing its first fiery breath. A frightening whoosh. In a flash the air all around was burningly hot. The flame-thrower operator pressed his trigger. The stream of blue and yellow flame shot forward. It seared and scorched all before it. As von Ostern watched in fascinated horror, the rod of flame slapped around the tower. For a moment it was wreathed in flames. When they vanished, the paint on the walls had begun to bubble and melt like the symptoms of some loathsome skin disease - and the machine-gun, glowing a dull-purple, hung there silent and useless.

'*Prima*!' von Ostern yelled excitedly and waving his pistol, added, 'Forward you flame-throwers! Come on now - we've got them on the run!'

Bent double like men advancing against a fierce wind, the flame-throwers lumbered forward towards the entrance, firing their awesome weapons, burning and scorching all before them, turning the road into an area of blackened smoking concrete. Here and there the defenders felled one of the operators, but the others pressed on triumphantly, knowing their weapon had caught the French by surprise and that they had to keep up the pressure.

Like primeval monsters breathing fire, the streams of flame shot out time and time again, ringing the towers and lashing the big concrete door with their searing heat. Now above the roar of the flame, von Ostern could hear the screams of agony coming from the men trapped in the towers and knew it was time for the engineers to carry out the next phase of the operation. He grabbed for his pistol and shrilled three blasts upon it. It was the signal for the engineers.

Papa Pontivy heard those three blasts above the moans of the terribly wounded men from the towers, as they were helped into the interior of the fort: charred moaning scarecrows, limbs oddly contorted, teeth gleaming a brilliant white against the black skulls of faces. He knew there was no hope for them. But he wanted them down in the sick bay away from the horrified gaze of the rest of the garrison. For he guessed that whistle signalled the main attack on the entrance. With his one hand he grabbed the phone from the wall bracket and yelled above the screams and moans of the badly burned men tottering by him on the underground road, 'Mercier - *vite*! They're using flame-throwers' - he heard Mercier gasp with horror at the other end and cursed him inwardly for doing so. The men were jittery enough; he didn't want his second-in-command to get nervous – 'and making progress. They've knocked out the two approach towers. My guess is that they'll make an assault on the main door soon. Prepare to seal off each unit at my command and ready a counter-attack force on the main road. Understood?'

'Understood, *mon Commandant*,' Mercier cried, his voice quite definitely shaky. 'And you sir?'

'I'll clear the casualties and take charge of operations here,' Papa replied, realizing suddenly that in spite of the fact the fort was defended by eight hundred men, its actual defence depended upon him. A quarter of a century of socialist propaganda and fortress mentality had sapped the courage of the ordinary French soldier. These sons of the men who had fought at Verdun lacked the determination and bravery of their sires. They needed a tight rein, or they would soon go to pieces. 'And Mercier,' he added swiftly.

'Sir?'

'Shoot anybody who refuses to obey an order *instantly*!' We need discipline now. Out!'

'*Oui mon Commandant*!' Mercier replied, but the phone was already dead.

Listening on the attachment, Walter paled. Flame-throwers, he told himself in horror. *They were using flame-throwers* . . . Anything was better than being burned to death with those terrible weapons . . . *Anything!*

Now the Rebels, doubling smartly behind their horses down the tight road packed with running grenadiers, could hear the vicious snap-and-crackle of the small-arms battle quite clearly. They could see the vivid flashes of ugly purple light, too, as the flame-throwers belched flame over and over again. The French, they told themselves, for they had no breath for conversation, were taking a beating.

A machine-gun opened up to their front – probably from the higher, secondary line of gun turrets. White-glowing tracer hissed towards the grenadiers. It scythed away the front rank, leaving them screaming and writhing on the unfeeling concrete. Polack didn't hesitate. There was no time to stop if they didn't want to become victims themselves. He slapped the nearest horse - hard. They bolted over the wounded, the wheels bumping and shuddering as they rolled over the young men, tormented eyes staring in accusation. Karl blinked back his tears. 'Sorry, comrades,' he gasped, 'sorry, but we couldn't help -'

His words were cut off brutally by a second burst of fire. Another group of running grenadiers skidded to a halt as they ran into that maelstrom of lead. They went down on all sides, clawing the air, desperate faces turned beseechingly to those cold silver heavens in the moment of death, as if pleading for God's mercy.

But God had gone away and hidden Himself this cruel dawn. There was no mercy for either friend or foe. God had abandoned his creatures, left them to their murderous games . . .

'Splendid . . . splendid!' Von Ostern urged the surviving engineers on, as they emerged from the smoke, carrying their charges, here and there springing over the dead who littered the approach road everywhere now. He wiped the blood from the side of his face and indicated the door only thirty metres away now and totally silent; for the flame-throwers had done their work well. The cost had been high, for they were all dead or dying by now, but they *had* silenced the door's defences. 'Knock on that door for me, engineers. Knock on it hard!'

A burly sergeant minus his helmet grinned and doubled forward, safe from the secondary line of machine-guns in the dead ground. Like a schoolboy playing tag he slammed his sticky bomb onto the door with a metallic boom and then doubled back the way he had come.

Wordlessly every one ducked. There was a muffled roar. The great door shook and quivered like a live thing as the hollow-charge bomb exploded. For a moment their view was obscured by a dense cloud of smoke. When it cleared, a delighted von Ostern could see that the charge had ripped a great jagged hole in the metal. 'Next man,' he cried above the racket. *'Los . . . der Nächste!'*

Another engineer bolted forward. He was not so lucky as the burly sergeant. A tiny black egg came sailing in from above. It dropped on the concrete, hissing furiously. The man stopped running and stared at it stupidly.

'*Hit the dirt, Schmitz* –' the burly sergeant began.

Too late! The grenade exploded in a flash of violent red. Schmitz flew back. His skull seemed to erupt. It flew apart, gore and bone bursting out of his head, as his face cracked and disintegrated, as if glimpsed in a breaking mirror.

The terrible sight shocked the engineers into immobility for an instant until the burly sergeant cried angrily, 'Oh, give me the frigging things!' He grabbed two of the bombs from the others and pelted forward once more. Another grenade sailed in from above. He aimed a swift kick at it. It sailed into the air and exploded in the drainage ditch. 'Gunners cover that roof!' von Ostern shrieked, realizing that his other company had not reached the top of the fort. Immediately the grenadiers began sweeping the area above the door with a wild outburst of angry firing as the sergeant crouched and slammed his bombs against the door. Then he was running back wildly the way he had come, his arms working like pistons, going all out.

'Come on . . . come on . . .' von Ostern urged him on. 'There's a piece of tin* in this one for you, Sergeant! Come on –'

The noncom had faltered in mid-stride, face wild with shock. His back arched as tight as a bowstring. His hands clawed the air, and then he smacked into the ground in the very same instant that the two charges exploded in a great echoing rending roar that seemed to go on for ever . . .

Von Ostern waited expectantly till the smoke had cleared. Suddenly tears of joy welled up into his eyes. Through the

*Slang for a medal.

drifting wisps of acrid yellow smoke, he could see the door had buckled and was standing half-open. The way ahead was clear! The brave sergeant had not sacrificed his life in vain. He hesitated no longer. Raising his bulbous signal pistol into the air, he fired the green flare: the signal for the men on the roof of the fort to begin coming down. He would need every single man he could find to force the road towards the command post, which was the brain and heart of Fort de Gambsheim. Then he swung round and cupping his hands he bellowed above the racket coming from the top of the fortification. 'All right, you grenadiers . . . Come on now . . . *Or do you heroes want to live for ever?*'

Karl groaned with despair. They were trapped again. Hitler and his damned military had got them. If they stayed where they were, the French gunners on the roof would slaughter them mercilessly; if they obeyed Major von Ostern's command and went forward, again they would be involved in the rotten business of killing their fellow human beings. 'Shit . . . shit . . . shit,' he cursed, beating his clenched fist in impotent rage against the side of the goulash cannon, 'the bastards have got us by the dong agen! What the frig are we gonna do?'

'Don't ask questions, that's what,' Ami said determinedly, as fresh grenades came sailing down from the roof in a lethal hail. 'Those frog pricks up there are gonna kill us dead if we don't frigging well get out of here – right sharpish . . . Come on!'

Polack lashed the horses' gleaming flanks and then they were off after the others clattering along the body-strewn road, knowing with sinking hearts that there was no way out for them. High up above them in his steel-clad observation tower, the look-out reported excitedly to Walter in the control-room, in his excitement forgetting to use French. Instead he choked in his native German, '*Walter . . . Walter . . . they're trying to get some sort of cannon into the fort . . . They'll massacre us . . .*'

Walter swallowed hard. First flame-throwers, now cannon. Surely they didn't stand a chance!

CHAPTER 6

VON OSTERN pressed his body tightly against the side of the buckled door. '*Now*!' he cried and tossed the stick grenade inside. The grenadiers behind him did the same and waited. A muffled crump. A blast of hot air. The door quivered against their bodies and then von Ostern cried, '*Inside*!' and they were tumbling into the fort, the enemy machine-guns already chattering from the steel gate beyond, eyes seeking frantically for some cover as the tracer raced towards them in a solid white wall. The Fourth Grenadiers were inside Fort de Gambsheim. The third phase of the battle had begun.

Rushing forward with the rest through the door into the cavernous yellow-glowing gloom of the entrance, the Rebels were caught in a furious burst of machine-gun fire coming from their right. Slugs howled off the metal skin of the goulash cannon, as grenadiers went down on all sides, galvanized momentarily into frantic electric action, as the bullets ripped their flesh to shreds. One of the lead horses was hit. It reared up in its traces like a highly-strung thoroughbred instead of the tame old nag it was, scarlet blood arcing from its wounded flank. The team panicked. The reins were torn from Polack's hands. The horses raced instinctively to the left to escape that murderous fire and just as instinctively the Rebels followed them: a move that saved their lives. For in that same instant, the massed French machine-guns behind the steel grille, which barred the road to the command post, concentrated on the new attackers, mowing them down mercilessly, while von Ostern, lying behind the cover of the miniature trains, screamed orders helplessly.

'*Crazy . . . crazy*!' Polack yelled, as they raced after the panicked team, springing over their own dead, blundering in and out of the place's equipment and abandoned wagons, ignoring the stray bullets which came winging their way. The team smashed into a makeshift barrier of packing cases, erected by the retreating French. The cases splintered. They could hear the goulash cannon smack into them. The wounded horse went down on its hindlegs. The others, still crazy with fear, tried to run on. To no avail. The weight of the dying horse was too much for them. It whinnied pitifully, the blood spurting from its wound, as they gave up, flanks quivering and lathered in sweat; and then suddenly they were calm, all fight gone out of them, simply standing there panting, their heads drooped in defeat.

A moment later the Rebels had reached them and were hacking at the traces with fingers that felt like clumsy sausages, trying to free the dying horse before the French spotted them. The Rebels had done it again. Now they were the only ones of the invaders not pinned down by enemy fire. And they were not slow to make use of their opportunity to escape that slaughter. Taking his rifle and pointing it at the dying horse's head, Karl closed his eyes and fired. The horse started up and in the same instant that it died, mercifully killed by that single bullet, they were urging the team on towards a narrow opening at the side of the cavernous entrance. A moment later they had vanished into the yellow darkness, leaving their trapped comrades behind them . . .

•

'Now listen, Mercier,' Papa Pontivy rasped, his old face drawn and ashen underneath the harsh glare of the naked electric bulb, 'we're holding them here. But a group of them, apparently armed with some sort of cannon, has managed to escape into communications Tunnel B.'

Mercier, at the other end of the phone, gasped at the mention of the cannon, while behind, Walter, listening at the extension, bit his bottom lip to prevent himself crying out in naked fear.

'I want you to round up enough men – I don't give a damn where you get them from – and put in an immediate counter-attack. I want Tunnel B clearing *at once*! Is that clear?'

'Yessir!' Mercier snapped, wondering who he could use. The Alsatians in the command post were definitely very jumpy; it wouldn't take much to start them running now.

'Another thing. If the Boche haven't cut the external lines, call Division. I want those fat bastards up there to do something too.'

'What, sir?'

'Immediate artillery fire brought down on the roof of the fort. I want the Boche reinforcements swatted off the roof like a cow driving off the flies with its tail!'

'But that's impossible, sir,' Mercier objected. 'We don't know if the roof could withstand that kind of fire. It should in theory, but in practice –'

'Listen to me, Mercier,' Papa cut in brutally, his voice savage and bitter now, as he realized once again just how weak and indecisive this new generation of Frenchmen were. They had bred a nation of weaklings between the wars. 'We hairy-assed old men did it in the Old War. You can do it in this war.' He chuckled suddenly, but there was no warmth in the sound. 'And if it doesn't work and the roof gives in, well, they'll give you a hero's funeral. Now get to it, Mercier!'

Miserably, close to tears of self-pity, King Bull crouched with the rest of the cooks, in dead ground on the fort's roof listening to the muted sound of the firing from below, wondering why suddenly the gun turret facing them had been retracted.

That old arse of a CO had come bursting into the rear echelon, waving his frigging sword as if he were about to lead a charge, crying 'Every man to arms! They are in desperate straits beyond the river. No time to waste. Immediate reinforcements are needed. Cooks, clerks, drivers – everyone. *To arms now!*'

As if in some horrible nightmare, from which there was no awaking, struggle as one might, a terrified King Bull had found himself transported across the Rhine, rushed through that lunar landscape, littered with dead grenadiers, to find himself now exposed on the roof of the damned fort, waiting for the crazy CO's order to attack. And why had that gun turret which had held them up so far, so suddenly retracted?

What was going on?

It was the same question which Colonel von Heinersdorff had asked himself, before dismissing the matter as of no importance. In the two and a half centuries in which the von Heinersdorffs had served Germany, they had never been given to introspection. They had sired the next group of officers, gone off to war dutifully, and had their thick heads obediently blown off without giving it all too much thought. Wasn't the family motto after all, '*Duty and Deeds*'? Now Colonel von Heinersdorff decided it was time to move on once more; the obstacle had been removed. '*Duty and Deeds*', he repeated to himself and then rising, he waved his broken sword, crying, 'On we go, my brave grenadiers. The back door has been forced. *Advance!*' He pointed the sword across the roof of the fort, just as he had done on the River Bzura in Poland when he had succeeded in having half the regiment slaughtered.

King Bull moaned miserably. What had he done to deserve this? Hadn't he kept the best kitchen in the Division, perhaps in the whole of the *Wehrmacht*? Wasn't he the inventor of the goulash cannon? What was an inventor, one could even say an artist in the preparation of food, doing up here, risking his valuable life with these ordinary common stubble-hoppers? It wasn't fair.

Von Heinersdorff beamed at him and his reluctant cooks. 'Come on *Oberfeld*. No lagging. Into the fray. I know just how much you and your chaps are eager to help our comrades below.' He laughed stupidly and at that moment King Bull would have dearly loved to have smashed his big fist into the Colonel's dotty face. But already the CO had moved on, waving his absurd sword.

Cautiously the cooks rose to their feet and began to advance once more, only too aware that there were hundreds of enemy soldiers metres below their reluctant feet. For a while King Bull, nervous and trembling, feeling naked and exposed on this bare, shell-pocked hilltop, thought they were going to make it in spite of the crazy colonel. But that wasn't to be. There was a sudden baleful scream. A trembling of the air. To the west, in the direction of Strasbourg, the horizon lit up a brooding eerie red. The keening grew louder and louder. King Bull stopped, the small hairs at the back of his bullneck suddenly erect with fear, his legs abruptly turned to water. He felt he would faint at any moment. The noise was almost ear-splitting now. King Bull opened his mouth, gasping for breath, face suddenly crimson red, as if he were being strangled. The world seemed to be racked by that terrible shriek. He fell to his knees, hands clasped together and raised to the heavens, as if he were praying.

Next moment it happened. The whole weight of massed divisional artillery slammed onto the roof of Fort de Gambsheim with one great roar. The fort rocked like a ship in a heavy sea. The hillside creaked and groaned, as if in protest at this terrible punishment. Men reeled dead and shattered on all sides and as if by magic great steaming holes appeared everywhere, concrete dust spurting from them so that in a flash the whole hillside disappeared in a thick grey acrid fog.

Screaming silently in absolute, overwhelming terror, King Bull stumbled forward, hand held out in front of him like a blind man groping his way, already sensing the hot wetness of his inner leg, for he had evacuated his bowels in his fear. Bodies were everywhere, writhing and tossing in their death throes. He didn't care. All he wanted was safety, anywhere to get away from this place of terrible slaughter.

Another salvo of shells screamed down. King Bull felt himself lifted, as if by some invisible hand. 'No . . . no . . . no!' he shrieked in his misery, 'please don't take me . . . *Oh, God please let me . . .*'

Then abruptly he was falling, falling, falling and the blackness was so profound that he no longer knew whether he was alive or dead, falling straight to hell itself . . .

Captain Mercier waited impatiently while his command post

signallers sought their equipment and put it on. Real Frenchmen, like little Bojax from Lyon, were eager enough, already waiting excitedly for what was to come. But the locals were being deliberately slow, flashing furtive glances to one another, as if they were just waiting for one single Alsatian to throw down his rifle in disgust for all of them to do the same.

'*Allez*,' he urged yet once again, as the minutes ticked, '*vite . . . vite, copains*!'

Walter, the senior operator, hesitated, his long face white and uncertain.

Mercier realized instinctively that this was going to be his trouble-maker, the one who might start the ball rolling. 'Corporal Walter,' he barked, 'why are you hanging around like that?'

Walter licked suddenly parched lips. 'It is difficult, sir,' he stuttered, as above them the roof trembled and the plaster rained down in a thick cloud. 'My mind,' he touched his temple, 'the noise and the –'

'*Nom de Dieu!*' Mercier cut him short angrily, 'what are you – some goddam woman having her damned periods or something? Move, when I say so, *move*!'

'But sir, what are we going to do against –'

'Hold your damned stupid trap!' Mercier yelled, his own nerves threatening to go at any moment, his hand flashing down to his pistol holster. 'Time is running out. Now move your arse, *sale con* – or else . . .'

The threat worked. Muttering to himself in dialect, Walter picked up his rifle and moved towards the door. The others followed, while Mercier watched them, hand on his pistol butt. Then he too went out into the yellow corridor, telling himself the vital counter-attack had failed even before it had commenced . . .

CHAPTER 7

NOW THAT tremendous barrage had ceased. The fort had stopped rocking and trembling, with the concrete dust falling in a thick grey rain. Cautiously, with Karl in the lead, and Polack and Ami following with the goulash cannon, they started to steal forward once more. Why they did so, not one of them could have answered at that moment. Perhaps it was because there was no turning back. Perhaps a young man's sense of mystery and adventure. Whatever it was, the three of them stole carefully down the tight tunnel, almost noiselessly. Even the horses seemed to be affected by the mood of the place; for they were silent too.

A dark shape loomed up out of the yellow gloom. Karl flashed up his rifle, startled. But with a scamper of clawed feet it was gone the next instant. It was only a rat. They went on, the sound of the fire-fight at the entrance vanished altogether.

They might as well have been the last men alive in the world.

Now the fetid, overheated atmosphere of the fort, its air supplied and warmed by a filtration plant, seemed to be growing cooler. Karl, at the point, swore he could feel a faint breeze on his sweat-lathered, anxious face. Were they close to some sort of exit or other? Gripping his rifle more tightly in sweat-wet hands, he advanced more rapidly. Perhaps they could escape from this damned tomb after all.

There was the sudden clump of heavy boots. Karl's heart missed a beat. '*There's somebody coming*!' he hissed.

Ami grabbed the lead horse, as Polack and Karl flattened themselves against the wall, hearts beating like trip-hammers. The sound came nearer. Polack rested his rifle carefully against the wall and clubbed a fist like a small steam shovel. 'Best do it this way,' he whispered urgently.

Karl, nerves trembling electrically, nodded his agreement. Hastily he pressed himself even closer to the wall to allow the big Pole more room.

The French soldier swung around the corner the next moment and stopped dead. For one long instant they stared at each other motionlessly. Then abruptly the Frenchman brought up his carbine, mouth open to shout the alarm. Polack sprang forward. With both hands he grabbed the Frenchman's weapon, bringing up his knee cruelly into the man's crotch. His yell ended abruptly in a thick throaty gurgling, as the shock of that cruel blow to his testicles forced his false teeth to bulge from his gaping mouth.

Polack grunted. He wrenched the carbine from the man's hands as if it were a toy and as the Frenchman bent to clasp his injured genitals, face contorted with the unbearable agony, Polack slammed his fist into his jaw. The Frenchman went out like a light. As his knees buckled, eyeballs already rolled upwards, Polack caught him. Gently, almost tenderly, he lowered the unconscious French soldier to the floor. 'Poor bastard,' he whispered. 'Fancy putting old fellows like him in the line.'

As an afterthought he bent down again and shoved the man's false teeth back into his mouth. He shook his head, as if sorely troubled by the injustice of this world, and they went on. Now the air was definitely becoming much cooler and fresher. Karl's hopes mounted. There was a way out after all. There was no need for any further action. He quickened his pace. The others, too. Even the tired old nags reacted. Their heads came up and their muffled hooves stepped out more briskly. 'I've got some of King Bull's precious coffee – real bean coffee,' Ami chortled. 'None of yer ersatz nigger sweat. Once we're out of this rathole, we'll get the old goulash cannon going and brew ourselves a canteen of real coffee, thick enough to stand a spoon upright in.' He smacked his lips in gleeful anticipation. 'Shit on shingle, my mouth tastes like a frigging gorilla's armpit! I'm going to sink a whole litre of the stuff!'

'Let's get out of this rotten dump first,' Karl began, as the thunder of cascading concrete, followed by the snapping metal roof supports, burst dramatically into his warning, and a cloud of thick choking cement dust swept down the tunnel to meet the Rebels.

Above them a deep crack zig-zagged the length of the roof like a monstrous zip-fastener. They stumbled to a halt and cowered against the wall, hands held protectively against their faces, coughing like ancient asthmatics in the throes of a final attack.

The crack grew ever wider with an alarming speed. The horses whinnied in absolute terror, eyes bulging from their sockets, as if they might well burst out of them at any moment. Now the crack had become a chasm. Dust and earth poured from it. The noise was ear-splitting, a kind of monstrous slithering and rending. They tensed, expecting the roof to fall in on them at any moment. Ankle-deep in dust now, the sweat-lathered flanks of the terrified nags covered in a grey mantle, they waited for the inevitable end, as Polack babbled the Act of Contrition in Polish.

A final rumble. A great slithering of displaced soil and in a shower of rock and dirt, a massive object slammed to the earth right in front of their feet.

For what seemed an age the noise went on and on, echoing and re-echoing down the dark chambers of the fort. Karl coughed and spluttered, feeling he was drowning in dust, his eyes screwed tightly closed, like small child trying to blot out the horror of a nightmare. Now slowly he began to open his eyes, hardly daring to believe that he was still alive.

Above them there was a gaping hole through which he could just glimpse a patch of pale grey sky, a long way off. In front of them the tunnel was littered knee-deep with boulders mixed with grey, dust-covered soil, in which rested the massive object that had fallen with the other debris in that dramatic cave-in.

Suddenly it stirred. Karl gasped. '*Boshe moi*!' Polack yelped and crossed himself hurriedly, while Ami clung to his other arm, whispering unnecessarily, '*Why . . . it's moving . .* !'

Moving it was. Slowly the object raised itself up like some grey ghost rising from the tomb, the dust showering from it. It gave a soft moan, while the three young men stared at the apparition transfixed. What looked like a grey skeletal claw reached out to seek something. It touched the front, the claw patting up little puffs of dust. What seemed to be a human visage appeared, as the thing gave off soft eerie moans, which sent a cold finger of fear tracing its icy way down Ami's spine.

And then there it was – a human face, bruised and battered, thick black blood caked on the nostrils and ears, but recognizably, definitely human!

The thing moaned miserably yet once again, and said in those well-remembered tones, though now they were humbled and softened by the humiliations and sufferings of this first day of total war, 'Dear God in heaven, please tell me where I am . . . Please God . . .'

As one of the three awe-struck young men cried, '*King Bull . . . IT'S KING FRIGGING BULL . . !*'

Papa acted, as the fresh Germans started to pour through the buckled door to the fort and the looks on his men's faces told him just how demoralized most of them were. 'Gas grenades!' he yelled. 'Use the gas grenades!'

Here and there the men hesitated, even his loyal Frenchmen. This secret weapon was illegal. Division had ordered it should only be used as a final resort in the most extreme of emergencies.

With his one hand, Papa pulled the pin of his own grenade. 'If we win we're heroes!' he cried. 'If we lose, we're war criminals. *Now throw!*' He grunted and lobbed the grenade towards the advancing Germans, clambering over the bodies of their own and the French dead.

The little egg exploded with a soft plop. Almost immediately thick grey smoke started to cloud from it with an angry hiss. Von Ostern, wounded for the second time, and weakening rapidly, fell to his knees, grasping at his throat. Weakly he tried to grab the grenade and hurl it back the way it had come. To no avail. The gas was too strong. His lungs felt as if a red-hot poker had been thrust into each one of them separately. Tears began to blind him. He ripped at his tunic collar. He was choking to death. The killing fog rose higher. A thin pink foam formed at his lips where he had begun to bite them in his desperate agony.

As in a slow motion film, he saw men sinking to their knees on all sides, disappearing into the fog of death, clutching at their throats, fighting the gas that tore and ripped their lungs apart. With the last of his strength, the red fires blazing in front of his bleared eyes, as he fought and wrestled with death, he waved the survivors to get back, to escape to the clean air. But already they were falling back, clawing and tearing at each other in their panic-stricken haste to escape before it was too late. Von Ostern gave one last sigh and slumped forward dead, his head lying in a pool of his own vomit.

Wearily Papa Pontivy waved his arm and shouted above the agonized cries of the dying Boche, as they sank into the gas, 'Enough . . . *assez!* . . . *assez!*'

Here and there the lone grenade sailed towards the Germans, but his men, too, had seen enough of those tormented faces, features crimson, heads twisted grotesquely to one side, tongues hanging out like strips of purple leather. They stopped their throwing, suddenly exhausted, breath coming in short sharp gulps, as if they had just run a great race.

Papa wiped the sweat from his brow. Next to him one of his men was vomiting wretchedly, sobbing at the same time, overcome by the horror of what had just happened. Papa frowned. He didn't like it either. Hadn't he been horrified, too, back in '16 when he had seen their own gassed soldiers struggling back down the support trenches at Verdun: long lines of blinded men, stinking of the mustard gas which had destroyed their eyes, stumbling through the mud, hands on the shoulders of the men in front of them, led by a medical orderly, who, in turn, sobbed and vomited just as the *poilu* next to him was doing? He wasn't heartless.

But when *la belle France* was in need, he told himself grimly, as the wind started to disperse the gas to reveal the grotesquely contorted bodies which littered the floor of the entrance now, one could not be squeamish. Any measure was justified, even the use of poison gas.

'*Mon Dieu*,' the soldier who was vomiting said thickly, startling him from his reverie, 'not that!' And then in German. '*Es ist unmenschlich. Das kann man nicht machen. Himmelherrgott!** He pointed a hand, which shook violently, in the direction of the door.

One of the 'dead' had risen and was crawling blindly towards them, face crimson, his lips chewed to a bloody cud in his unbearable agony, dripping blood as he crawled.

'He's coming for us!' another cried, voice bordering on the hysterical. 'For what . . . we've done to him.'

'Let's get out of here!' a third yelled in panic. *'The dead are rising!'*

The dying German came crawling on, meaningless sounds coming from his shattered throat, a kind of unbearable ecstasy on his contorted face, as if for some strange reason, he was actually *happy*.

The *poilus* edged back in terror, muttering among themselves. Papa heard the clatter of a rifle being dropped on the floor. In a minute, he knew they'd break and run. These were not their fathers' children. They were a bunch of lily-livered petticoats. Suddenly overcome by a burning rage, Papa Pontivy fumbled for his pistol, as the lone Boche crawled ever closer and the terrified muttering among his soldiers rose. He jerked the pistol out and clicked off the safety catch. His men flashed worried glances from him to the Boche and then back again. Papa cursed and took aim, as if he were standing on some peacetime range. The foresight dissected that horrible face. Papa took first pressure. Behind him someone cried, 'Don't shoot . . . he's dying as it is . . .'

'*Sale con . . . salaud* . . !' Papa cursed and pressed the trigger. The pistol jerked in his fist. But the bullet didn't miss its target. The Boche howled miserably, as his face split apart and he was flung back against the wall by the impact at such

*'It's inhuman. You can't do that. Good God!'

short range. For a moment he hung there, as if he were fighting for every last second of precious life. Then he slumped forward, dead.

Papa swung round on his cowed men, eyes blazing with fury. 'Listen, you excuses for men, that is the only way to treat the Boche. Kill them! The only good German is a dead one, remember that. Now, don't stand around there with yer fingers up your idle arses. Get moving. Start building up the defences again. And move it, the Boche if I know him at all, will be back soon enough. *Move!*'

Reluctantly they started to restore the defences of the entrance while Papa glared at them, pistol still held in his one hand. The slaughter of that single Boche had done it, he told himself. They would hold now until the Division counter-attacked and restored the situation outside. There was only one catch. That damned cannon somewhere to his rear. If Mercier did not succeed in eliminating it, the trouble would start all over again. He stared at his reluctant soldiers and then at the German dead packing the entrance. A country's greatness, he told himself, depends on the readiness of its menfolk to sacrifice themselves for the cause. The Boche had been prepared to do just that, for they had a cause, however perverted it might be: National Socialism.

His men were different. They remained farmers, shopkeepers, clerks and the like in uniform, who had no other cause than saving their own worthless skins and returning to their comfortable, purposeless civilian lives. They had no dream of the glory of France. Papa Pontivy sighed and felt very old and weary. He had fought for his country ever since he was eighteen. Suddenly he realized that all that sacrifice, sweat, and blood meant nothing. His France had died on the battlefield at Verdun in '16; this new France of his men was alien to him.

Papa Pontivy sighed and wished he were dead . . .

CHAPTER 8

'I CAN'T . . . I can't go on,' King Bull moaned and started to drop once more.

Ami aimed a savage kick at his big rear. 'Get moving, you big prick!' he cried. 'We're nearly out of here now. Now get moving.'

Tamely the big NCO accepted the kick, as if he were some dumb beast of burden which had known nothing but cruel blows all its life. The old King Bull seemed to have vanished.

They staggered on, the old nags picking their way carefully through the concrete rubble and soil which littered the tunnel. At regular intervals they could glimpse the sky through the holes in the roof the French shells had made during that terrible bombardment. But they were too high up for the horses and they were determined not to abandon them or the goulash cannon. King Bull's invention, which he had hoped would keep him out of the fighting, had grown upon them. Somehow or other they were going to get it and the nags out of Fort de Gambsheim, cost what it may. And all the while, Ami egged them on with his delightful vision of 'real bean coffee with the spoon standing upright in it!' They followed it as they might have done the Holy Grail.

Now they began a slight incline and Karl reasoned that the tunnel, in which they found themselves, might be one of those which led to the surface observation posts. If it was, then they were in luck. Outside the bombardment had ceased. They might be able to make it safely back to the Rhine, using King Bull as their excuse; if anyone stopped them, they were bringing back a wounded superior. And the big prick was certainly knocked about. His face was swollen to twice its normal size and now he sported two very black eyes. His nose had suffered too. He had turned a peculiar green colour and seemed well off centre. 'Couldn't have happened to a nicer feller,' Karl told himself with a wry grin,as he watched the ragged NCO stagger on, shoulders bowed as if he bore all the cares of the world. At last King Bull was being paid back for all the insults and injuries he had inflicted on the three Rebels.

Now the incline grew steeper. The nags dug their hooves in, twin streams of grey coming from their nostrils as they exerted more energy. 'Here, you, plush-ears!' Ami, who seemed to have taken charge of King Bull, barked. 'Put your idle shoulder to the goulash cannon and give the horses a bit o' help!'

'But I hurt,' King Bull objected. 'I hurt all over my face and shoulders, honest.'

'You'll hurt up yer frigging fat ass!' Ami snorted, 'if you don't do as I say smartish.'

Wearily King Bull placed his big paws behind the cart and began to push as the horses laboured steadily up the incline.

It was when they had almost reached the top, King Bull grunting and alternately blinking back tears of self-pity, that it happened. The little black egg came rolling and clattering down the slope to meet them in the same instant that the frightened voice cried in German, '*Surrender . . : or you die*!'

It all happened so startlingly that Karl had no time to be afraid. Instinctively he picked up the hissing grenade and flung it upwards in the direction from which it had come. There was a cry of alarm, followed by one of rage, as the grenade exploded and Karl yelled, 'Come on, quick . . . or else they'll slaughter us down here! *Los Kameraden!*'

The three Rebels darted forward, leaving King Bull standing there behind the goulash cannon staring in open-mouthed bewilderment, too dazed to be afraid.

The three comrades swung round the corner. A Frenchman lay slumped against the wall, bleeding from nose and ears. He was conscious. Another knelt there, moaning piteously and staring down in horrified disbelief at his two stumps. His hands lay in front of him like abandoned white gloves.

'Up there – up the corridor!' Polack yelled, as a slug smacked into the wall close to his bullet head. He jerked up his rifle and fired from the hip without aiming. The French who had fired the shot ducked behind cover hastily.

Karl thought quickly. They were going to have to make a fight for it, if they were going to escape from the fort, but with a bit of swift action they might make the French run for it. He whipped the stick grenade from his boot, pulled the pin and lobbed it forward, crying in the same instant, 'Bring up the cannon, Sergeant Bulle. *Los mit der Kanone!*'

The noise was ear-splitting as the grenade exploded in those close confines. The Frenchman who had fired at Polack screamed shrilly. In a blast of orange flame, he was blown against the opposite wall to hang there flattened and dead like a cardboard figure. Karl doubled by him, followed by the others. Now they could hear the excited gabble of voices round the corner, some in French, the rest surprisingly enough in German. The enemy were Alsatians, Karl told himself excitedly, and he renewed his cry to King Bull, hoping his trick would pay off. '*Where's that cannon? . . . At the double, Bulle . . .*'

Ami grinned suddenly, as he realized what Karl was up to. 'Smart-ass!' he yelled, as Polack loosed off a magazine to keep the French behind cover.

'Somebody's got to use his turnip in this outfit!' Karl yelled back as Polack's slugs howled and richocheted off the walls, striking up a fury of blue sparks.

Then they could hear the clatter of horses' hooves, muffled by the rags, but definitely coming closer. King Bull had heard Karl and was obeying orders. The goulash cannon was on its way to battle.

Walter heard the clip-clop of the horses, too, and the cries in German. Ashen with fear he took his gaze off Bojax, dying in the corner, his guts spilled out into his blood-filled hands, and looked at Mercier.

The young captain was pale, too. The swift German reaction to their attempt to ambush them in the tunnel had shocked him. His first taste of action had come a sharp surprise, too. Yet he was still prepared to fight on, pistol gripped in his hand, jaw set. But the young fool didn't realize what a cannon-shell could do in these tight confines. All it needed to do was to strike one of the concrete walls to turn the place into a death trap, with cement and shrapnel flying everywhere, flaying their bodies mercilessly.

Again that harsh demand for the cannon to be brought up echoed and re-echoed down the tunnel. Walter's nerve finally broke. 'Captain Mercier,' he quavered urgently, 'don't you know what they're doing down there – *they're bringing up a cannon* . . . It'll take only one shot and we're as good as dead.' He repeated his words in German and the locals broke out in an excited chattering, eyes flickering from the tunnel to the pale-faced captain, as if willing him to make that overwhelming decision – and make it soon.

'What do you think I should do?' Mercier asked, realizing for the first time in his young life that he was being expected to make a decision that could save or destroy human lives, perhaps even his own.

'Surrender!' Walter snapped harshly. 'It's the only way.'

'*Surrender*!' Mercier echoed horrified, face aghast. Surrender was a word that had not been present in the dictionary at St Cyr.* Cadets from there either won the battle or died heroically in the midst of the fighting. 'But I can't . . . do *that*!'

'You can,' Walter urged, seeing that Mercier was weakening. 'The odds are too great. You have no other alternative . . . Sir, let's not waste any more time. Once they start firing that cannon, we're lost.'

'*Ja, ja*,' the others agreed, forgetting their French for good now. '*Wir müssen schnell machen!*'

As if to emphasize that he would fight no more, Walter dropped his rifle with a clatter to the floor. The sound startled Bojax. He lifted his head and took in the scene at once. 'Sir,' he groaned, face contorted with the unbearable pain of his wound, 'don't . . . don't do it.' His plea ended in a burst of

*Famous French military school.

thick coughing, and black blood began to trickle down the side of his mouth.

Mercier looked helplessly from the dying soldier to the rebellious, frightened Alsatians. 'But –' he commenced.

'No buts!' Walter interrupted harshly, knowing that the officer was weakening now. 'What does it matter whether we fight on or not? Germany will win this war anyway. France is too weak, governed by a bunch of communist Godless Jews. Our Führer deserves to win . . .'

Mercier gawped, stunned by the mention of 'our führer'. Slowly, very slowly, he began to lower his weapon knowing he'd receive no more support from this bunch of turncoats and traitors in the uniform of the French Army.

Walter gave him no opportunity to change his mind. His right hand lashed out. He wrenched the pistol from Mercier's nerveless fingers, crying out in German the next instant at the top of his voice so that the attackers down the tunnel would be able to hear, '*Heil unsern Führer, Adolf Hitler*!'

While an ashen-faced Mercier stared at them in shocked disbelief, the other Alsatians clicked to attention and shot out their arms in the Nazi salute, crying as one '*HEIL HITLER*!'

Karl reacted immediately, taking in the situation at once – the cowed officer, the enthusiastic, smiling Alsatians, who had already ripped the insignia of the French Army from their uniforms, the tall blond corporal, bearing a white towel as a token of surrender. He snapped, 'All right . . . all right, you're safe . . . we'll accept your surrender. Now this is what you'll do . . . You, Corporal . . ?'

'Walter!' the Alsatian clicked to attention woodenly, as if he were a Prussian guardsman. 'The name is Walter, sir!'

Karl shook his head in disbelief. 'All right, Corporal Walter, I want you to double back to that control room of yours –'

'*Sofort*!' Walter barked and turned, as if to go immediately.

'Hold your piss!' Karl cried, irritated by the man's fawning manner, 'Go to your control room and contact all your units. Tell them the fort has surrendered. Tell them that everyone is laying down his arms and they have to do the same. Tell them that all fighting has ceased. *Tell them that Fort de Gambsheim is German!*'

Thus it ended without any more blood being shed. They had killed and been killed. They had become savage animals and those who had survived, victors that they were, knew secretly that they were condemned. Sooner or later the god of war would claim them.

Now they watched as the cowed prisoners were herded away, past the old, one-armed French officer who had shot himself in the moment of surrender, down to the Rhine and the cages beyond, disappearing into the mist. Everywhere green signal flares were shooting into the darkening sky indicating German victory.

But the 'Goulash Cannon Heroes', as Colonel von Heinersdorff had acclaimed them happily as they had emerged from the fort with their prisoners, felt no sense of victory. The cost had been too high. For now the victors were following the vanquished, dragging their feet wearily, wrapped in silence, a handful of grey ghosts out of the many who had started so confidently. They were high-spirited boys no longer. Their youthful yearnings, which had stirred their blood easily, had vanished in the rage and despair of battle. They had become veterans, soldiers. Doomed men, all.

Sombrely Karl took the trace and cracked the leather rein. Wearily the old nags began to shuffle after the infantry. Behind them *Fort de Gambsheim*, ruined and captured at last, was left to the dead. Wordlessly, each man wrapped up in a cocoon of his own thoughts, Polack and Ami followed as the first black shadows started to slip in over that lunar landscape like silent black ravens from the east. The 'Goulash Cannon Heroes' were returning home . . .

Epilogue

'One of the greatest fallacies of our time is that the Nazis rose to power because they imposed order on chaos. Precisely the opposite is true – they were successful because they imposed chaos on order. They tore up the commandants . . . They said, you may persecute the minority, you may kill, you may torture, you may couple and breed without love. They offered humanity all its great temptations. Nothing is true, everything is permitted.'

John Fowles

It was 'Führer Weather'.

A beautiful, hot afternoon, with the sun's rays shining a dappled green through the ancient French oaks of the Forest of Compiègne. Near where the Fourth Grenadier Regiment was drawn up for inspection, the army engineers sweated still as they positioned the ancient *wagon-lit* for the great ceremony to come.

Here in that same coach on the morning of 11th November 1918, a beaten humiliated Germany had surrendered to the triumphant French and her allies. Now the Führer was coming to reverse that victory. After a brilliant six weeks' campaign, in which the French had been soundly thrashed and her English allies had fled the Continent, it would be France's turn this time to surrender.

It would be the greatest moment in Adolf Hitler's life.

At quarter after three, the stream of black Mercedes arrived in the glade. Colonel von Heinersdorff barked his command. What was left of the Fourth Grenadiers clicked to attention as one. Even the looted French horses, which now pulled the goulash cannon, stiffened, as if they too were aware they were in the presence of greatness. Now the *Prominenz*, Hitler, Goering, Himmler and all the rest who had engineered German's revenge, strolled towards the great granite block which the victorious French had erected here twenty-two years before.

Karl watched as Hitler read the inscription chiselled on it and Dr Schmidt, his gigantic interpreter, translated it for him: '*Here on the Eleventh of November 1918 . . . succumbed the criminal pride of the German Empire . . . vanquished by the free peoples which it tried to enslave . . .*'

Hitler turned to Goering, a look of absolute triumph on his face, and snapping his hands to his hips, brought down his right boot sharply like a proud farmyard cock after yet another sexual conquest.

The gross commander of the German *Luftwaffe* raised his bejewelled baton, as if in salute.

Now followed by his bodyguard of SS thugs, all heavily armed, hands on pistols, as if they half-expected some French assassin to pop out of the oaks at any moment, Hitler strode over to where the Fourth Grenadiers waited, standing rigidly to attention.

He and a proud von Heinersdorff, now sporting his new Knight's Cross around his neck, exchanged a few words, before the latter stepped back with a sweep of his sword. '*German soldiers . . . comrades*,' that harsh guttural voice echoed through the trees. 'You of the Fourth Grenadiers had the honour of being the first German troops to cross over to the soil of France since 1918. You were the tools of my great plan . . . the oath I swore as humble soldier, half-blind and wounded back in that terrible November . . . that I would avenge Germany's horrific defeat . . .'

Karl standing next to the goulash cannon with the rest of the cooks under a proud King Bull, no longer listened to that rasping bitter Austrian voice. He had heard it often enough in the past and it sickened him. Instead he concentrated on the face of this new master of Europe.

To him it seemed an ordinary face, save for those eyes: big, bulging and completely mad. They were the demented eyes of a man who had deliberately chosen evil. Now he and the rest of his fellow Germans were condemned to serve this monster to the bitter end; for he knew that his march of conquest would not stop here in this pleasant French wood. There were new countries to be conquered, new peoples to be subjected, new victories to be celebrated with the cruel cheap bombast of the New Order. As if challenging the very gods themselves, Hitler threw back his head, dark eyes blazing at the blue sky, and declared: 'I stand or fall in this holy struggle. I shall not survive the defeat of my people. *Comrades, Germans, we march and win – or we die!*' Karl shivered dramatically.

Now the Conqueror of France began to walk the length of the rigid ranks of grenadiers, followed by the CO and the newly promoted *Major* von Schorr. Eyes gleaming fanatically from that pudgy yellow face of his, Hitler exchanged a few words here, a handshake there, a paternal pat on the cheek for the boyish replacements, until finally he reached King Bull's cooks grouped around the bubbling goulash cannon, giving off the scent of thick pea soup. For a moment his smile seemed genuine, 'A goulash cannon,' he whispered enraptured, as if he were remembering that time when he, too, was a humble infantryman. 'Cooking thick green pea soup.'

'Half a litre per man, *mein Führer*, made of best *German* peas,' King Bull, whose burly chest was now adorned with both classes of the Iron Cross, assured him proudly, emphasizing the '*German*' peas, as if it were important.

'Excellent, excellent!' Hitler enthused. 'Nothing is too good for my brave soldiers . . . in a regiment where even the cooks win awards for bravery in the field.' He gazed at Karl, whose chest bore the Iron Cross, First Class, too, and frowned momentarily, as if something in the young man's fierce gaze did not quite please him. Then he dismissed whatever he was thinking and said, once more in high spirits, 'Goulash cannon heroes, the lot of you. Splendid work, head cook. Keep it up!' He extended his hand and for a moment an astonished King Bull was allowed to submerge the flabby paw of the most powerful man in Europe in his own massive hand.

Then the band was thundering, all blaring brass, the clash of cymbals, the thumping bass of the big drum, the rattle of the kettle drums. And what was left of the Fourth Grenadier Regiment, the Crown Prince's Own, was marching by their Führer, arms pressed rigidly to their sides, eyes fixed unswervingly on some distant horizon, boots slamming down on the cropped turf in the goose-step, marching away to the new battles to come.

Now the goulash cannon to the rear of the parade started to draw level with the rostrum. The French horses were frisky, made nervous by the clash of the cymbals and Polack had to exert all his strength to keep them under control. '*Eyes right*!' Karl commanded.

The three Rebels clicked their heads to the right as one, as they sat bolt-upright on the little cart. Beyond the rostrum they could see the line of French vehicles approaching. They would bring the tired old beaten French generals to sign the surrender. Suddenly Karl felt very sorry for them, for all the peoples of Europe who would have to surrender to that monster up there.

Hitler's stern look vanished. He turned and cracked some joke with Goering. The latter rumbled with laughter, his heavy jowls shaking. 'The goulash cannon heroes will win us this war yet, *mein Führer*,' Karl heard him exclaim quite distinctly. 'Any army where the cooks win medals for bravery is unbeatable!' Again he raised his baton, the jewels flashing in the sunlight, as if he were saluting them.

And then the goulash cannon heroes were gone, trailing the odour of 'fart soup', made of best German peas, behind them . . .